THE HOBBIT ™

THE BATTLE OF THE FIVE ARMIES

OFFICIAL MOVIE GUIDE

THE HOBBIT™

THE BATTLE OF THE FIVE ARMIES

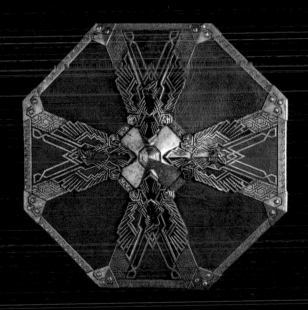

OFFICIAL MOVIE GUIDE

Brian Sibley

HarperCollins*Publishers*

HarperCollins*Publishers*
77–85 Fulham Palace Road,
Hammersmith, London W6 8JB
www.tolkien.co.uk

Published by HarperCollins*Publishers* 2014
1

Photographs: Todd Eyre, James Fisher, Nels Israelson, Grant
Maiden, Mark Pokorny & Steve Unwin; Angela Randall
(page 97); Rex Features (pages 141 & 154)

Editor: Chris Smith
Design: Terence Caven
Cover design: Stuart Bache
Production: Kathy Turtle

A catalogue record for this book is available from the
British Library

ISBN 978 0 00 754414 1
ISBN 978 0 00 754413 4 (Signed Limited Edition)

Printed and bound in China

CONTENTS

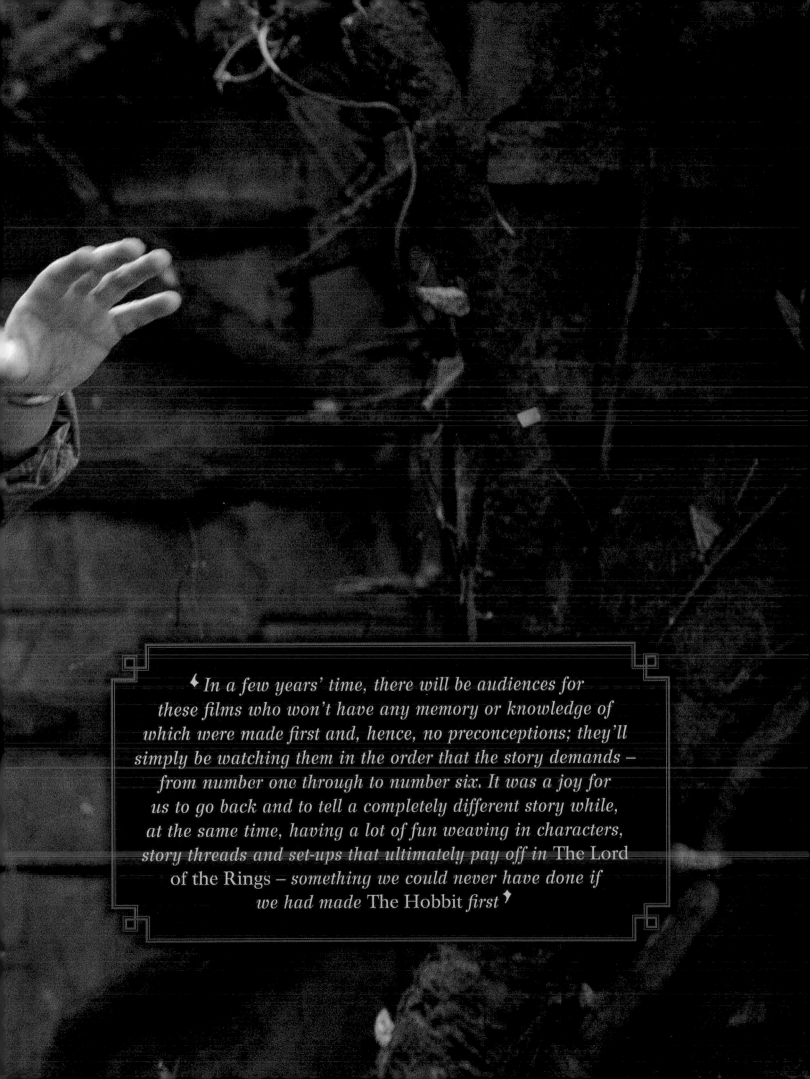

In a few years' time, there will be audiences for these films who won't have any memory or knowledge of which were made first and, hence, no preconceptions; they'll simply be watching them in the order that the story demands – from number one through to number six. It was a joy for us to go back and to tell a completely different story while, at the same time, having a lot of fun weaving in characters, story threads and set-ups that ultimately pay off in The Lord of the Rings *– something we could never have done if we had made* The Hobbit *first*

HOBBIT-FORMING

'IT'S A UNIVERSAL STORY,' IS HOW PETER JACKSON DESCRIBES J.R.R. TOLKIEN'S *THE HOBBIT*. 'IT'S THE STORY OF A DISPOSSESSED PEOPLE, ENDURING MANY HARDSHIPS IN THEIR ATTEMPT TO RECLAIM THEIR HOMELAND AND OF THE GREED AND MADNESS THAT OVERTAKES SOMEBODY WHO WANTS SOMETHING ALMOST TOO MUCH. AND, IN THE CHARACTER OF BILBO, IT IS THE STORY OF AN INNOCENT WHO IS FUNDAMENTALLY CHANGED BY THE EXPERIENCE OF GOING ON THIS TOTALLY UNEXPECTED JOURNEY.'

It is also, of course, a precursor to Tolkien's later epic tale, as Peter explains: 'Something of the essence and ingredients of *The Lord of the Rings* is there in *The Hobbit*, but it is just mixed in a slightly different way. It's a little more humorous and you could say the characters are a bit more colourful, but it's a strong story with its own epic quality: it has spectacle – amazing landscapes and visual splendour – and there's no shortage of action, adventure and excitement.'

Having already successfully explored Tolkien's world in the *Rings* trilogy presented Peter Jackson and his colleagues with a challenge: 'We wanted *The Hobbit* to be the same filmmakers going back into Middle-earth, shooting a movie in much the same style, but the story and characters are different so that inevitably gives it a different flavour. It is more naïve and lacks the same cataclysmic struggle between good and evil that is the central theme of the later book. Nevertheless, it has a strong narrative and many of the events are establishing the fact that forces are at work that will later play a major role in *The Lord of the Rings*.'

The clearest link between the two works is the Ring, which Bilbo finds in Gollum's cave under the Misty Mountains and which gives him the power of invisibility, enabling him to aid the Dwarves when they find themselves in various difficult situations. Only later did the author come to realize that Gollum's 'precious' was nothing less than the One Ring of Power made, lost and sought for by the Dark Lord, Sauron.

'It is only when you read *The Lord of the Rings*,' says Peter, 'that you realize the extent to which Bilbo's adventures in *The Hobbit* have changed him as a character. The Ring slowly

LEFT: *Director Peter Jackson and Martin Freeman discuss Bilbo's next scene in Erebor.* OPPOSITE: *Where Tolkien had sketched the characters of the Dwarves, the filmmakers would need to create fully developed characters who the audience could care for as the story progressed.*

❧ It is only when you read The Lord of the Rings *that you realize the extent to which Bilbo's adventures in* The Hobbit *have changed him as a character ❧*

becomes a great burden for him. Not only that, but he never really settles back into hobbit life and – as far as his fellow hobbits are concerned – he is treated with a degree of suspicion because he carries the stigma of having gone off and had wild adventures in foreign parts and, they all suppose, is now living in a hobbit hole crammed with pots of gold.'

Discussing Tolkien's literary style in *The Hobbit*, Peter says: 'I find it fascinating that at the time Tolkien wrote *The Hobbit* he was inventing a bedtime story for his children and had no knowledge of the events that were to befall in *The Lord of the Rings*. However, the simple tale was in fact just a relatively innocent prologue to an epic saga with a darker tone.'

The nature of the book as a children's entertainment full of episodic incidents presented the filmmakers with a further dilemma, as Peter explains: 'Tolkien wrote *The Hobbit* at a breathless pace and was more concerned with getting to the next exciting event than with stopping to develop the characters. When you attempt to turn that material into a movie, made in a style worthy of being a companion to *The Lord of the Rings*, a sequence that may have taken only a page or two in the book can easily become ten minutes of film footage.'

And that process of giving the characters greater depth whilst still being faithful to the original narrative proved interesting for the team: 'You discover that the story absorbs those elaborations rather like a sponge absorbs

water! It has an ability to grow and yet still be *The Hobbit* everyone knows and loves.'

This goes some way towards answering one of the most frequently made comments with regard to *The Hobbit* trilogy: 'It's interesting,' says Peter; 'people say, "Well, it's a relatively slight novel so how come it's three movies?" What you have to understand is we're not just adapting the original *Hobbit* novel. Once *The Lord of the Rings* was written and published, Tolkien realized that the sequel revealed various inconsistencies or blanks in *The Hobbit*. So he always intended to revise what was now a prequel in order to tie up those loose ends.'

Indeed, in 1951, fourteen years after first publication, Tolkien made a few changes for a second edition including rewriting the 'Riddles in the Dark' chapter in order to give the 'true' version of how Bilbo came by Gollum's magic Ring. Originally Gollum had wagered his precious possession on the outcome of the riddle contest, but Tolkien now had Bilbo, instead, find it by chance. However, many

LEFT: *Bilbo's theft of the cup would be the catalyst to drive the story on in both the book and the films.* ABOVE: *Many significant features in the film trilogy, such as the appearance of the human settlement of Lake-town, would adhere closely to Tolkien's original conception as written and illustrated by him.*

other questions remained unanswered, such as where does Gandalf go when he abandons Bilbo and the Dwarves on the edge of Mirkwood, and the true nature of the mysterious 'Necromancer'.

In 1960, Tolkien tackled the problem again, as Peter explains. 'He was intending to re-write *The Hobbit* to link up to the events in *The Lord of the Rings* as well as to give the story a more "adult" tone, but, after only a few chapters, Tolkien abandoned the attempt and it was never finished. However, much of the material he never got round to writing can be found in a set of Appendices that were published at the end of *The Lord of the Rings*.'

These Appendices provided the structure for the Jackson *Hobbit* and contributed to the growth of what were originally two films into a trilogy. 'In adapting *The Hobbit*,' says Peter, 'we wanted to have it talk directly to *The Lord of the Rings*, 'so, using Tolkien's notes as our blueprint, we created a more expanded version of the story that you read in the novel itself and to some degree we're doing what Tolkien wanted to do but never did.'

A result of the trilogy being filmed across an extended period of time has given the films an unexpected synchronicity with the experience of the characters in the story: 'A typical movie,' observes Peter, 'would shoot for three or four months, but our filming took place across more than a year which, interestingly, is the same period of time that it takes Bilbo to travel 'There and Back Again'. So, as it turned out, the making of the movie was almost like walking step-by-step, stride-by-stride with our company of characters as they fulfilled their quest.'

THIS PAGE: *While the set dressers finish adding detail to the set, Peter prepares for the next part of the shoot outside the Front Gate of Erebor.*

Direct Action: Thoughts on PJ as Director

T ALK TO ANY CAST MEMBER ON *THE HOBBIT* AND YOU BEGIN TO BUILD A PICTURE OF WHAT IT'S LIKE TO BE AN ACTOR IN A PETER JACKSON FILM. ASK JED BROPHY, WHO PLAYS NORI, AND HIS REPLY IS UNEQUIVOCAL: 'HE IS A GENIUS WHO HAS THE GENIUS TO SURROUND HIMSELF WITH GENIUSES, SO YOU'RE NOT JUST WORKING WITH HIM, BUT WITH PEOPLE WHO ARE THE BEST IN THE WORLD AT WHAT THEY DO.'

More specifically, Jed focuses on Peter's unique understanding of story and character: 'He not only comprehends how the different races and creatures interact, he also really understands the climactic beats of the story and how to push actors towards those beats. He quite simply knows every character's emotional arc better than any other director with whom I've worked. He can tell you exactly where your emotion should be in any scene at any moment because he's got it all in his head.'

Ian McKellen, now in his sixth movie as Gandalf, also marvels at the director's seemingly effortless ability to keep on top of so many aspects of his filmmaking: 'I am amazed at the rate Peter works: five or six days a week and, if you're directing a movie, then you're there from the minute the day starts right through to the end and beyond, because there are decisions that are having to be made regardless of whether it's lunch hour or the end of the day. And yet, you never see a moment when Peter doesn't have the energy needed for whatever a situation may require. He spends a lot of every day sitting and waiting. But the mind is always whirring.'

'He is carrying so much around in his head,' says Graham McTavish, playing Dwalin. 'I asked him, once, how he did it. We were working on the second film at the time and he said, "Oh, I've always been good at carrying films in my head. Having said that, I don't have the Battle of the Five Armies in my head just yet, but I *do* have the next four, five, six weeks." Extraordinary. And he still manages to be the king of enthusiasm. Considering just how much is on that man's plate it's remarkable that he is always so enthusiastic, cheerful, funny and sensitive

to what other people are feeling. Not only that, but, regardless of the fact that he is directing a film with a budget of many hundreds of millions of dollars, he'll still find time for a joke because he recognizes how important it is to make the people in front of the camera feel relaxed.'

Agreeing, Gloin's Peter Hambleton notes: 'The working atmosphere is very focused, disciplined and rigorous but the opportunity to laugh is vitally important because it releases tensions, and out of the right sort of relaxation some of the best acting often comes.'

'Pete's a big kid,' is how Evangeline Lilly puts it. 'He knows how to keep things light. Not only that, but his background in gore and horror means that he loves all the blood and guts and stunts.' That said, the actress playing Tauriel also recognizes the Jackson determination to pursue excellence: 'He's fearless and won't rest until things are perfect; so, as an actor, you are always protected and never worry that you'll end up with "egg on your face". Being able to trust my director while, at the same time, being able to "play" and have fun are important to me, which is why working with Peter is such a treat.'

That sense of reliance on Peter's judgement is something that Ian McKellen also values: 'I never feel as if there's too much at stake when I'm with Peter. I can trust him. He'll know when he's got from me what he needs to make a scene work, so that leaves me free to just get on with doing my best.'

Not that the director is shy in offering directions, as Thorin's Richard Armitage reveals: 'Peter gives you subtly nuanced guidance, which isn't necessarily what you would have originally thought but which fills you with confidence that you're in safe hands. There have been many times when I've felt as if I was on very shaky ground and really didn't know what I was doing. But Peter knows this film and Thorin's character better than I do, and so, because of my confidence in him, I do something I've never done before with a director, I just hand it all over to Peter and let myself be guided.'

A tireless search for different ways of playing a scene is a Jackson trademark: 'Very often,' says Peter Hambleton, 'he will tweak a moment so that it is, maybe, a little bit kookier, darker or more ambiguous. He has an ability to find another colour or flavour in any particular moment, to see how we can mine it a bit deeper with a view to having many more choices at his fingertips when he's at the editing stage. To me that's why he is a great director: despite the pressures of time and money that are always at his shoulder, he can still have the nerve and the courage to go for an even sweeter take in terms of drama, humour or emotion.'

For Adam Brown in the role of Ori, the aspect of the Jackson directing method that was most appreciated was his willingness to allow actors the freedom to try an approach of their own: 'He is so easy and approachable that you can go up to him and say how you feel about this or that and he's always ready to listen and talk about it. Depending on the scene, he will happily leave a lot up to the cast to decide where our characters are going. He has a great way of letting us think that we're discovering something for ourselves although, of course, he's already thought through all of the options a hundred times before we've even started, but he always lets us get there in our own way as actors.'

Bifur's William Kircher pursues this idea: 'It's no fun working with a director who doesn't know what he wants. And the thing about Peter Jackson is he *really* knows what

he wants and yet he still welcomes your input. You go to him as a director with thoughts about your character – "What if I were to do this… or, maybe, that…?" and if it fits with his vision, he'll say, "Great! Let's do that!" But even if it *doesn't* fit with how he sees things, he won't say, "No,": he's more likely to say, "Yes, we can try that, and maybe we can try it this way as well…" So, behind the freedom to explore there is still a very clear understanding of where it should be going.'

'Working with Peter,' says John Callen as Oin, 'is an interesting process. He appears to be a very unassuming director who never yells and screams and who understands the value of what everybody else is contributing to

BELOW: *Peter surveys the debris outside the Front Gate with Martin Freeman, while Ken Stott reviews Balin's next lines.* (Inset) *The director shares a special moment with William Kircher, Graham McTavish, Peter Hambleton & Stephen Hunter.*

the film. But that doesn't mean that he doesn't push for high standards. He most certainly does. And if there are things that aren't quite meeting his vision of what these films should be, then he will pursue them until that vision can be achieved.'

'And if he pushes you,' puts in Jed Brophy, 'you don't get to just do a couple of takes and hope it will be alright, Peter will keep shooting until he gets the magic in that shot that he's looking for which, as an actor, is exactly what you want – to be challenged. Every day is a challenge working with Peter: you get pushed to the very limits of what you can do as an actor and I think there's nothing better than that because that is how you get better at what you do.'

'Peter loves pushing everyone to the maximum,' says Stephen Hunter, playing Bombur, 'in order to get what he wants. He is really focused on getting the very, very best in each shot, no matter how many takes we do. Sometimes that's hard, but he always manages to do it in a way that makes you want to be working even harder and harder!'

'Communication,' says Peter Hambleton, 'is one of the really strong aspects of what Peter brings to the filmmaking process. His communication is incredibly clear and precise and he explains everything in a way that gives you a sense of where you are in the story. A good actor needs context, "Why am I being encouraged to play this moment this way? How does it connect to everything else?" Having answers to those questions gives you a much better chance of delivering the results that everyone's after.'

For Aidan Turner, one of the pleasures of being in *The Hobbit* has been the 'organic' way in which the script developed: 'When we began filming I could honestly say that I didn't know what would be happening to Kili: what scenes would be written or how I was going to play them. Sometimes filming can be a bit frightening when everything is set in stone because you have to keep your finger on that pulse in case you make choices about how you play a scene that later clash and can't be changed. But now I'm a big fan of leaving things open to a certain degree, and then just letting them unfold.'

Sometimes the words of the script are not just open for interpretation but accessible for rewriting as Ryan Gage

discovered in playing Alfrid: 'Peter will often say, "Oh, you know, say something like this or that…" and leave it up to you. He likes to keep it as free as possible. In one respect, it's all tightly scripted, but at the same time – if he gets an idea or you get an idea – it can also be *un*-tightly scripted!'

Such an approach can take some getting used to, as John Bell, playing Bard's son, Bain, discovered: 'The most challenging thing I've found is having to take Peter's ideas and make them reality because he's got so many and he fires so many at you. You can easily be taken aback by it, but he is just trying to get you to come up with ways of playing a scene. You can feel like you're dry, like you've given all that you can give, but he'll offer you that wee boost and then something will happen. You'll think, "Wait, I can try it this way," and – *boom!* – suddenly it all works together.'

John Callen reflects on the fact that Peter Jackson wasn't initially going to direct *The Hobbit*: 'He created *The Lord of the Rings*, gave us a physical representation of that book and those characters in a way that's obviously unique. So it seems only right and fair for the world of film-lovers that he came back to do *The Hobbit*. And I think it was fortuitous for us, to say the very least, that he did.'

'Middle-earth *is* Peter Jackson,' adds Jed Brophy, 'and without Peter Jackson there would be no Middle-earth! He has created the fabric and the texture of the cinematic Middle-earth and I couldn't imagine anyone else directing *The Hobbit*.'

'It's great to see him at work,' says Ken Stott, playing Balin, 'because he has such energy for it. And his enthusiasm rubs off and makes long days short. What a fantastic position Peter is in – almost like a deity in charge of this world, which is his Middle-earth.'

Or, as Ryan Gage puts it with a laugh: 'He's in his playground, really. He's got this amazing sandpit to play in and we're all his little toys! But, of course, in a great collaborative way!'

The last word should perhaps go to Beorn's Mikael Persbrandt: 'Peter Jackson,' he says with candour, 'is a director who has a universe of his own. I've met a few, and when you do there's not much to talk about. You're invited into this world of theirs and you just have to saddle-up and go along for the ride…'

GANDALF –
THE CONSTANT PRESENCE

GANDALF IS UNIQUE! NOT SIMPLY BECAUSE HE IS A WIZARD, BUT BECAUSE – WHETHER GREY OR WHITE – HE IS THE ONLY CHARACTER TO APPEAR IN ALL SIX FILMS THAT MAKE UP THE DOUBLE TRILOGY OF *THE HOBBIT* AND *THE LORD OF THE RINGS*.

'In many ways,' says Philippa Boyens, 'he is our navigator. He has the ability to understand both the detail and the larger picture. He is the alarm that is sounded: locating where the jeopardy lies and revealing the true forces that the rest of the world is up against.'

Not that his character – at least as Gandalf the Grey – is without conflicts and contradictions, although that, as Philippa points out, is part of his appeal: 'He's still very much of this world and susceptible to the mistakes that any of us might make. But through it all he is a guardian of Middle-earth who is always acting on behalf of others rather than himself.'

Although resembling a man – and appearing nothing more than an elderly wandering conjuror and firework-maker – Gandalf is a powerful Wizard and one of the Maiar, a group of spirits-in-human-form sent into Middle-earth to help oppose the might of Sauron. Known by the Elves as 'Istari' – or 'Wise Ones' – these Wizards were five in number and included Radagast and Saruman who, until his corruption by Sauron, was the head of their order. Tolkien tells us that Gandalf was the last to arrive in Middle-earth and, being old and grey and leaning on a staff, was assumed by some to be of little consequence. In truth, as is seen in his film portrayal, his aged, vagabond appearance concealed someone of great wisdom and strength.

'This odd appearance,' says concept artist, John Howe, 'is his disguise; appearing as the old, bent man in tattered travelling clothes is just the way in which he hides his power. Because of his image we accept that Gandalf has seen it all: the worst and the best, the pettiest and the grandest. He really is the Grey Pilgrim, the Wanderer, the one who can't rest, because, somewhere, something

important is always occurring. And so he becomes our guide, making sure that we, too, get a chance to go with him and see what is happening.'

Along with the consistency of Gandalf's presence across six films is that of the man who has come to embody the personality of the character, Sir Ian McKellen.

OPPOSITE: *During six films spent working together, Ian McKellen formed a close bond with Peter Jackson based on trust and mutual respect (top). Gandalf closely examines a priceless artefact (bottom).* THIS PAGE: *The unmistakable silhouette that will forever be associated with the Wizard.*

ABOVE: *The actor is presented with a portrait of himself as Gandalf the Grey to commemorate his final day on set.* BELOW: *Ian McKellen listens attentively while Peter shares his thoughts on Gandalf's next scene.*

'When a great actor inhabits a role,' says Philippa, 'they *become* that character, so that when you go back and read the book again you cannot imagine Gandalf as looking like anyone other than Ian; and, when you think of the films, you simply can't visualize anybody else ever having played the role.'

Alan Lee, who as an illustrator has created his own depictions of the character, agrees: 'Tolkien's description of Gandalf is rather vague and unformed, but now, when I open the pages of the book and I start to read a line or two of one of Gandalf's speeches, it is Ian McKellen's voice and face that appear in my head and I'm pleased about that, because he's just made such a wonderful job of creating this character that he now really *is* Gandalf.'

It is a sense of satisfaction which Philippa Boyens shares: 'It's not a bad day for a screenwriter to have Ian McKellen say your lines, because you can guarantee that whatever you thought they were going to sound like, they will be ten times better coming out of his mouth! And whatever you might have thought you had imbued them with, he will find something else – some other little nugget of understanding – that, in turn, inspires you.'

And, for Alan Lee, the McKellen portrayal of Gandalf is one destined to endure: 'From now on, people will always make the association between character and actor and it is a performance that is going to stand the test of time.

And that's to the benefit of the character himself because – without losing anything of Gandalf's supernatural element – Ian has brought real humanity to the part: irritable, impatient and bad-tempered and, at other times, kind, warm and sentimental.'

Summing up Ian's personality – much of which is now part of an iconic image recognized all over the world – Philippa says: 'He is young in spirit and yet, at the same time, incredibly wise. He is full of curiosity: every day is fresh for him, every moment is interesting, every line of every script is an adventure.'

FIRST STOP: BREE

The moment Peter Jackson steps out of a doorway onto a dark, rainy street chewing on a carrot in the opening shot of *The Desolation of Smaug*, fans of *The Lord of the Rings* trilogy knew exactly where they were – the village of Bree, which sits on the road between the Shire and Rivendell.

Here it was in *The Fellowship of the Ring* that Frodo, Sam, Merry and Pippin, on the run from the Black Riders, stopped for the night and, at the local inn, *The Prancing Pony*, they met Strider who would become their companion on the journey to Rivendell.

In revisiting Bree for the second instalment of *The Hobbit* trilogy, the filmmakers drew on J.R.R. Tolkien's Appendices to *The Lord of the Rings*, which mention a chance meeting there between Gandalf and Thorin. At this meeting their conversation touches upon the exile of the Dwarves from Erebor and the ever-present danger of Smaug the Dragon.

'We started in Bree,' says Philippa Boyens, 'for a number of reasons: not only was it a fateful meeting that gave us a chance to remind audiences what the Quest is about, but also because it reveals Gandalf's trepidation about what is happening in Middle-earth. He never assumes that the world is at peace. This is sixty years before the events of *The Lord of the Rings*, and whilst there is no great reason for immediate disquiet, Gandalf has a growing sense of unease, a sense of things taking place unseen that he does not know about.'

Among the anxieties weighing on the Wizard's mind is the Dragon, as Philippa explains: 'Gandalf understands that if there was to be an attack on the Free Peoples of Middle-earth it would come from the East or down from the North. But, more than that, and perhaps his greatest misgiving is, what would happen if Smaug were to be suborned and unleashed by an enemy? Imagine great armies of the Orcs setting forth, marching out to war, with a Dragon at their head. Absolutely devastating; game over!'

First readers of *The Hobbit*, back in 1937, would have been unaware of how this potential danger had helped initiate the Dwarves' attempt to recover their ancient homeland but it gave the filmmakers an opportunity to add another dimension to their story, albeit with one small amendment: 'In the book,' says Philippa, 'the meeting between Gandalf and Thorin is a chance encounter, but we needed the scene to be more dynamic, Gandalf to be more proactive. Sensing that now is the time to act, we had him hunt down and seek out Thorin. In so doing, however, he unwittingly forces the enemy to act.'

THIS PAGE: *Adorned in the raiment and golden armour of his ancestors, Richard Armitage as Thorin looks every inch the rightful King under the Mountain.* OPPOSITE: *Thorin's obsession to reclaim his homeland will see him isolated from friend and foe alike.*

Richard Armitage

THE NEW KING UNDER THE MOUNTAIN

'THORIN IS CANTANKEROUS AND PROUD; HE'S QUITE AN ANGRY, BURDENED CHARACTER.' THAT'S THE VERDICT OF RICHARD ARMITAGE, THE MAN WHO PLAYS HIM, WHO GOES ON TO SAY: 'BUT THORIN ALSO HAS A FIERCE SENSE OF HONOUR AND LOYALTY: IF YOU SHOW HIM YOUR LOYALTY, HE WILL EMBRACE THAT AND TRUST YOU. BUT IT TAKES TIME TO GET TO THAT POINT WITH HIM BECAUSE HE'S BEEN HARDENED BY LIFE, SO HIS OUTER SHELL IS PRETTY IMPENETRABLE.'

One of Thorin's biggest problems, says Richard, is his prejudice towards Bilbo: 'From day one when he walked into Bag End he was anti-hobbit! The fact is he's expecting a warrior when he gets to Bag End and, instead, there's a halfling. Gandalf rules that this character has to go along with them but Bilbo's a sort of thorn in his side, because Thorin knows that they're setting out on a dangerous mission and there's this niggling voice in the back of his head telling him that, sooner or later, they're going to hit trouble: this Mr Baggins is going to be a problem because he'll slow them down and hinder them. Thorin's frustration and fear is that he'll have to turn around and go back for him, or go out on a limb for him and try to save him – and that he *will* because, deep down inside, he knows that he wouldn't be able to let this guy fall. That, I think, shows a concerned and caring side to Thorin, but it's one that he resists because, being battle hardened, he can't afford to be seen as that person.'

However, as Richard notes, the relationship between Thorin and Bilbo is an evolving one: 'I think there are certain things that Thorin doesn't know or acknowledge about himself that, through Bilbo, he comes to realize. Also, the hobbit really proves himself during the course of the first film, and almost certainly every step of the way

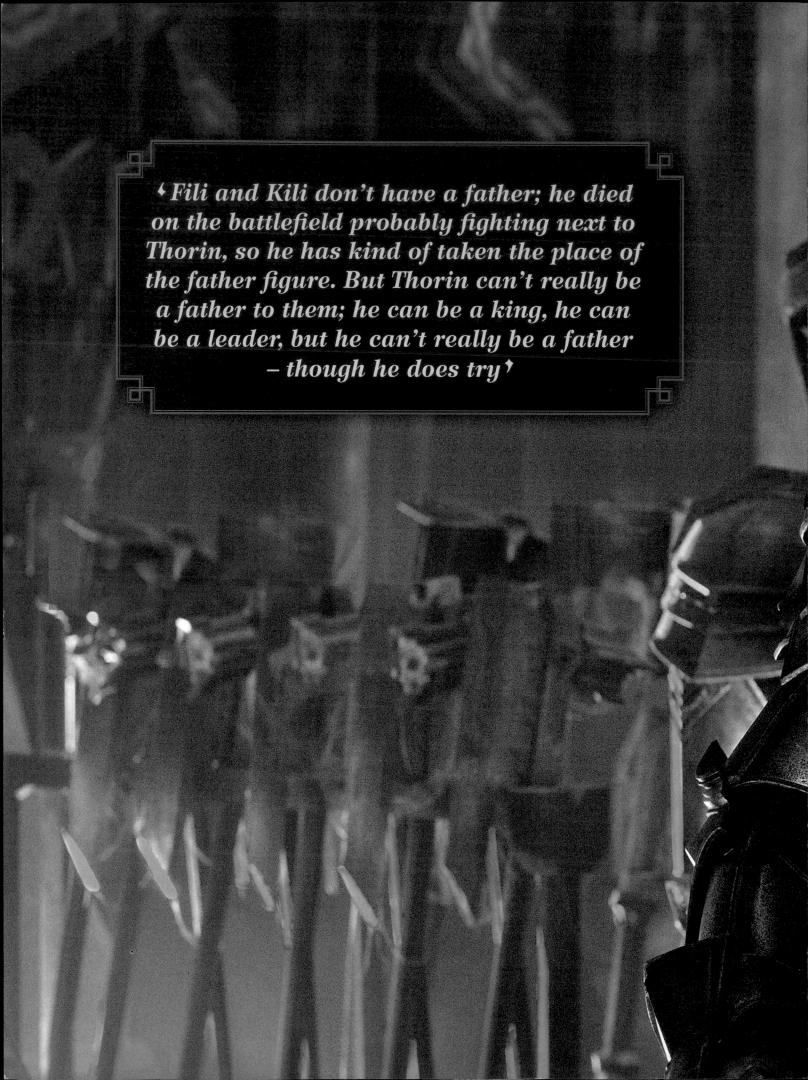

'Fili and Kili don't have a father; he died on the battlefield probably fighting next to Thorin, so he has kind of taken the place of the father figure. But Thorin can't really be a father to them; he can be a king, he can be a leader, but he can't really be a father – though he does try'

OPPOSITE: *Thorin Oakenshield, the warrior king, now wielding an ancient Dwarvish sword recovered from the armoury of Erebor.*
ABOVE: *Richard Armitage steals a quiet moment from the hectic production to reflect upon Thorin's dialogue.*

in the second film. At every stage throughout the course of the Quest Bilbo surprises him and that's where the relationship between them really thrives; because Thorin realizes that this little person is going to give him loyalty and this forces him to question his lack of trust in others. Only later will that loyalty will be seriously tested and the outcome have dramatic consequences for this unlikely friendship.'

Talking about another significant relationship in the story, Richard says: 'Giving the characters a background is very important in helping establish their believability. The fact that they have a history, that we know something about them, clearly informs the way we relate to them as the drama unfolds and that is particularly true of Thorin and Thranduil.'

The fact that when Smaug attacked the Lonely Mountain the Elves refused to come to the aid of the Dwarves is a significant event in the history of both races and the two characters. 'That one event,' says Richard, 'created irreconcilable friction between Thorin and Thranduil. So, when Thorin and the Dwarves are captured and incarcerated in the Wood Elves' kingdom that is a really difficult situation for Thorin to find himself in, because he believes that the Elves' refusal to help when

Erebor fell was because it was in their interest that the Dwarven kingdom was weakened. That is uppermost in Thorin's mind when he and Thranduil come face to face, and whilst his tactic is to lock down and say nothing, seeds of hatred and distrust are sown that will yield a devastating harvest in the third film.'

Underlying all Thorin's troubled relationships is his gradual yielding to the poisonous effects of 'Dragon sickness', as Richard explains: 'It's a lust for gold, an addiction that has a physical effect on a person and creates a psychosis inside them that everyone else is trying to take it from them. Thorin watched his grandfather suffer from Dragon sickness and he has a massive fear that he, too, will be susceptible to it. By the time he gets to the Mountain and is confronted with the extent of the wealth of Erebor, he realizes that he is already succumbing to the sickness. It is a fatal flaw.'

Richard approached the portrayal of Thorin's gradual surrendering to desire as an insatiable obsession: 'I am thinking of it as an addiction: once he's in the Mountain, he can't leave and the further he gets away from the gold, the more acute the illness becomes – and it's only when he is back close to it again that the craving is eased.'

Paint Your Dragon

'THERE IS NO SUCH THING AS A TYPICAL DRAGON.' THAT'S THE VERDICT OF ILLUSTRATOR JOHN HOWE, WHO HAS DRAWN MORE DRAGONS IN HIS TIME THAN MOST ARTISTS. 'CLASSICAL DRAGONS TENDED TO BE SNAKE-LIKE, OFTEN WITH MANY HEADS; MEDIEVAL DRAGONS CAME IN ALL SHAPES, SIZES AND PERMUTATIONS: TWO LEGS, FOUR LEGS, WINGS AND NO WINGS.'

Remembering the lengthy process that would eventually lead to the creation of Smaug in *The Hobbit*, John says: 'We doodled and drew and kept pecking away on and off for ages and ages until we had a Dragon… Characteristically, Peter was reluctant to settle on a final design until, in the terms of the script, he really needed to know what it would look like, so a lot of Dragoning went on for quite a while. Peter would nod and say, "Oh, yes, that looks interesting…" but you could tell that he wasn't ready yet to get down to brass tacks.'

Successfully capturing Smaug on film was, as Peter recalls, always going to be one of the biggest challenges in filming *The Hobbit*: 'There are certain iconic characters in movies where, from the outset, you have this understanding that unless you get this right you will be jeopardizing the entire film. I knew that our audience already had high expectations about what Smaug would be like and if we delivered a Dragon that, to some degree, didn't surprise and please people, then we'd be in big trouble. It was a double-edged sword: Smaug needed to be exciting *and* sort of scary!'

About one aspect, Peter had no doubt: 'The one thing I knew, going in, was Smaug's size. I asked myself what would make him more scary, and I just thought, he's big, massive, *huge* – way, way huger than what you would ever imagine. No reason why he can't be. Erebor's a vast place – there's plenty of room for him in there!'

That was true in the sense that it was someone's job to make sure there was enough room in Erebor for a supersize Dragon, as Assistant Art Director, Michael Smale, recalls: 'The scale of Smaug certainly influenced the designing of some of our environments. The Dwarven halls of Erebor had to be of a scale built for Dwarves yet, at the same time, vast enough so that Smaug could move through. The halls have geometric grids of columns and, within the Treasure Hall, the spacing of this grid was determined by it being of a width that Smaug could slither through using the columns as handholds. Similarly, in the early mapping out of Lake-town, we took a Smaug puppet and considered its relation to the size of the town. Our first version of the town was much

LEFT: *This design by Weta Workshop's Andrew Baker varies the size and appearance of Smaug's scales to convey his great size, and his age, before design work was handed over to Weta Digital.* OPPOSITE: *An early concept drawing by John Howe, which helped capture the essence of the Dragon.*

too small, and looked as though Smaug would be able to decimate it with nothing more than a few big swishes of his tail. The town needed to be of a size that it would take Smaug some time to destroy, and so was made much larger. The bigger canals needed to be wide enough for Smaug to be able to fly along their length, so their span was determined from the width of Smaug's torso.'

There were, notes John Howe, one or two other aspects to Smaug that were established early on: 'Peter said that Smaug was very old and was quite attached to the idea of an ancient Dragon with sagging, flaking skin and rheumy eyes. Obviously, we also knew he had to have wings because he has to fly and that he was to be a red-gold colour, just as Tolkien describes him in the book. Then, as Peter's vision for Smaug became more defined, he told us that he wanted a long, serpentine creature, so that we could have him "swimming" through the gold.'

There were weekly meetings of a group of key creatives who came to be known as Team Smaug and gradually – but slowly – the Dragon of the Lonely Mountain began to take shape. 'All we really knew,' says Weta Workshop's Richard Taylor, 'was that somehow or other Smaug needed to be the quintessential archetype of a Dragon. So a huge *pot pourri* of design ideas began to pour in from all angles and mustered towards a design conclusion.'

Reflecting on this time, Peter says: 'I find it reasonably easy to tell people what I *don't* like, but it's very hard to describe what I really *want*. So, instead, I try not to do that because, having so many incredible conceptual designers, you want to give them a degree of freedom. Yes, establish a few parameters – avoid this, avoid that – but then basically let them go for it. What I really love is having twenty different designs for Smaug, and then, whittling down from the big picture to smaller and smaller details, piece together a final image.'

'Peter was searching for a unique Dragon design,' says Weta Digital's Senior Visual Effects Supervisor, Joe Letteri, 'and achieving a combination of the different aspects he was looking for – the size, mass, wingspan – and a capability to do all the things that Smaug needed to do took a while to consolidate.'

A piece of artwork by Weta Workshop's Gus Hunter featured a Dragon with an upturned mouth which caught Peter's eye and chimed with something he already had in mind, as Joe remembers: 'Peter and Fran had come across some images of crocodiles which always seem to have this kind of sly smile, almost as if they are amused by the thought that they're about to eat you. Of course, that's just us projecting a human characteristic onto the reptiles, but it was an idea that appealed to the filmmakers and one they wanted to be a part of Smaug's character, so John Howe drew an element of a smile into the design. Later it would present us with the challenge of finding a way to avoid it looking as if he had a permanent grimace on his face.'

Crocodiles weren't the only reptilian inspiration, as Senior Texture Artist, Myriam Catrin, reveals: 'Other animal references used to help create Smaug were alligators, caimans, iguanas, Water Dragons, Bearded Dragons, Sumatra Flying Lizards, Blue-Tongue Lizards and Snapping Turtles, with an unexpected added component in the form of an aerial photograph of the dunes on Mars, which Joe Letteri came across and which had a polygonal pattern like the skin of a reptile. We refined it and used it to create Smaug's tongue and the thin membrane of his wings, so you could say that Smaug is partially from Mars!'

Meanwhile, the final shot of the first film, *An Unexpected Journey*, was to reveal Smaug awakening under his mound of treasure and opening an eye. 'The question then,' says Peter, 'was "how big is his head?" At that point, we didn't know exactly how big the rest of him was, but we were going to see his eye and his nostril

so we needed to make a decision. I said, "Well, it's got to be at least as long as a Greyhound bus," and people went, *"What?"* That was our starting point in terms of the size and scale of Smaug and a rare example of my saying something I *wanted* rather than *didn't* want.'

That took things to the end of what was by now the first episode in a trilogy, but that was clearly not the end of the story. 'The truth is,' says Peter, 'in that last shot you saw part of Smaug's head but there wasn't actually anything else under all that gold. For the next film, however, we needed to show more than just the Dragon's eye and, second time around, we had a little more time.'

However, *An Unexpected Journey* had also featured a prologue on the history of Dale and Erebor that required a few brief tantalizing glimpses of the Dragon. Recalling that first, fleeting manifestation of Smaug, Joe Letteri says: 'We concentrated, in those flashbacks, on his physical performance. The idea was that he had four legs, and wings attached to his back. We knew that that really didn't work as an anatomical structure, but Peter wanted a four-legged Dragon because we had these scenes of him stomping through Erebor and it gave him a certain strength.'

The question of anatomy, however, never quite went away, as John Howe explains: 'There came a day when Peter decided Smaug should only have two legs. He wanted to find a way of making the Dragon more interesting and menacing and one answer was to take away Smaug's front legs and change his whole physical way of moving. This was opportune because we had taken it about as far as we could design-wise, so we jumped back in, chopped off two legs, kept the head and the tail and re-drew everything in between.'

'The challenge,' says Joe, 'was in finding a way for the Dragon to give a convincing performance in the vitally important dialogue scenes with Bilbo: having four legs and with wings attached to his back really wasn't that helpful, because we wanted to use his hands, as an actor would. We achieved this by getting rid of the forelegs, attaching the wings to the arms and giving him an extra finger, so he had three fingers to control his wing membranes and another three human-like fingers for gesturing, grabbing and so forth.'

John demonstrates the effect by crushing his fingers into his palm and folding his hand back into a painfully distorted position so that his wrist-bone and knuckles are

⭐ *The staggering fact is that Smaug had over one million scales on his body, each and every one of which is some combination of being hand-modelled or hand-painted so that whilst they're similar, they're all unique* ⭐

THE OFFICIAL MOVIE GUIDE

thrust downwards: 'By folding his wings up like a vampire bat, Smaug can propel himself along on his "knuckles".' With a laugh, he adds: 'There's actually a lot of my hands in the shots of Smaug's because we studied them to get the articulation right.'

Whilst having spent a lot of time with reproduction skeletons of birds and bats around his desk, John confesses: 'We were less concerned with concepts of real anatomy than with what *felt* right. Essentially, it was less to do with creating a creature than with designing a character that happens to be shaped like a Dragon.'

Questions of anatomical feasibility were not quite as negligible as John suggests and translating the concepts into a functioning animal shape involved its own challenges, as Weta Digital Model Supervisor, Marco Revelant, explains: 'We had to solve how to connect the wings in a way that makes Smaug's ability to fly believable and we tested different solutions by varying the point at which the wings were attached to the body. In the end we used a muscle system similar to an eagle's, which seemed the most successful given the fact that the wings were doubling up as hands. The challenge with those hands – bearing in mind that there is only limited movement in Smaug's wrist – was to find a way to articulate the fingers without having the three long ones on the wing membrane crash into the body.'

Perhaps most demanding was the requirement that Smaug needed to be able to talk and convey highly sophisticated emotions. 'Our facial modellers,' Marco remembers, 'spent a lot of time trying to create a realistic network of muscles that could allow the scope of performance needed by the acting. We had to convey the feeling that the lips could have a wide range of motion without looking detached from the general structure. Also we had to make sure the opening and closing of the mouth was coupled with enough secondary motions such as the movement of the throat and how the surface of the skin would stretch and contract in a natural way as he speaks.'

The biggest challenge of all was the *bigness* of Smaug: whichever way you looked at it, there was an awful *lot* of Dragon to be handled. 'Some of the statistics and

ABOVE: *A close-up view of the Dragon's skin, showing the diversity of scales around the upper part of his head.* BELOW: *John Howe's design for Air New Zealand's Boeing 777-300 'Hobbit plane' would be scaled up to a 54-metre image that adorned each side of the plane, allowing Smaug to really fly.*

measurements of Smaug,' says Digital Modeller, Andreja Vuckovic, 'leave you speechless. From the beak to the tip of his tail he is nearly 140 metres. His head alone is six metres long with head spikes that are more than four metres in length, sixty-six sharp teeth in his mouth and an eye the size of a fifty-five-centimetre Pilates ball. His wing span is the equivalent of two jumbo jets and with his scaly skin you could cover a whole soccer field.'

That skin surface alone presented Weta Digital with a phenomenal challenge. 'The amount of detail that went into him,' says Joe Letteri, 'was tremendous. To begin with we needed to establish some idea of how big his Dragon scales were so that when you see him without another character in the scene you still have some clue as to his size. We had deliberately designed scales in fine detail so that, when you saw close-ups on his face, the skin could fold and wrinkle properly. As a result, the scales were very small but when you pulled back into a wide shot they were *too* small for the eye to register and virtually disappeared. So we integrated larger scales among the smaller ones, placed in such a way that the skin remained flexible but, when seen from farther away, you still knew just how big he was.'

This, as Joe reflects, proved a labour-intensive process: 'Because we didn't know which areas were going to be important until we saw how all the shots came together, we were constantly repainting him. If you were to ever get a really close-up look at those parts that you never see closely in the movie – such as the back of his legs or the tip of his tail – you'd see that there's an incredible amount of detail there. The staggering fact is that Smaug had over one million scales on his body, each and every one of which is some combination of being hand-modelled or hand-painted so that whilst they're similar, they're all unique.'

So how long does it take to paint a million scales? Textures Supervisor/Creative Art Director, Gino Acevedo provides the answer: 'It took the team six months, but it wasn't just a case of painting a million scales, we had to make sure that everybody's scales were looking like everybody else's scales, so that when it all came together the skin surface would blend and the scales have a really

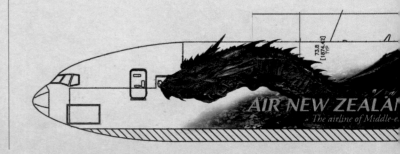

natural flow.' Laughing, Gino adds: 'As to what it takes to be part of a team painting a million scales, let me just say, they're all still going through therapy!'

One of the key aspects of Tolkien's description of Smaug is that the Dragon had lain so long on his pillaged hoard that his under body was studded with precious gems: 'What magnificence,' says Bilbo, 'to possess a waistcoat of fine diamonds.' The size of the movie Smaug had ruled out this embellishment, until, as Gino recalls, an enthusiastic fan viewing the trailer for *The Desolation of Smaug* posted that they thought they had caught a glimpse of the Dragon's bejewelled 'waistcoat'. 'So Peter says – and by now this is quite late on – "Well, that means that maybe we're going to have to look at doing that and getting some of the gold and stuff in there." And everyone's thinking, "Oh, no! All because of one fan!" But, you know, we did it and it worked and looked beautiful. In the shot where Bilbo is looking up and sees that Smaug has a missing scale you can see a lot of that encrusted gold.'

In order to help humanize Smaug, Weta Digital worked with Smaug's voice talent, Benedict Cumberbatch, on creating a sense of performance, especially in his scenes with Bilbo, as Joe explains: 'We brought Benedict in and had him in a motion-capture suit with a facial camera rig so as to understand what his body and face were doing when he delivered Smaug's lines. We've done a lot of motion capture and it works very well if you're creating a humanoid character like Gollum, but you can't really translate an actor's performance directly to a Dragon. What we were able to do, however, is to study the subtleties of movement that Benedict gave to the performance: how a tilt of the head revealed that he was intrigued by something that Bilbo was saying, or how, when he got angry, he would thrust his chin forward or

DRAGON BOOTS

'A vast red-golden Dragon,' was Tolkien's description of Smaug, but the question facing the filmmakers was *how* red and what *shade* of red? 'A lot of concepts were being done working with the colour red,' recalls Textures Supervisor/Creative Art Director at Weta Digital, Gino Acevedo. 'We knew it had to be a specific kind of red that would look realistic, something that you would see in nature. Obviously nature has some pretty wacky stuff, like poison arrow frogs, which are almost fluorescent, but we were open to all kinds of possibilities – even a pair of red cowboy boots that Visual Effects Supervisor, Eric Saindon, came across online! Dyed leather with an interesting texture and a nice buffed feel to them, they were, probably, one of our more unlikely inspirations for Smaug.'

pull back defensively. These are the moments that we looked for in order to translate the ideas behind the design into the character you see on the screen.'

Having achieved so much, one irritating inconsistency remained: the fact that those prologue scenes still featured a four-legged Smaug. A solution was presented through the planned release of *An Unexpected Journey* Extended Edition on DVD, for which Weta Digital 'retrofitted' the new Smaug into the old shots. Even within the mythical world of Dragons history can get re-written!

THE LURE
OF DRAGON LORE

'**T**HIS DRAGON HAS GOT A SEVERE PERSONALITY DISORDER!' PETER JACKSON IS TALKING SMAUG. 'I MEAN, HE'S NOT JUST A DRAGON WHO CAN TALK, AND WHO WANTS TO EAT PEOPLE, HE IS ACTUALLY A PSYCHOPATH!'

'Yes,' agrees screenwriter, Philippa Boyens, with a laugh, 'he *is* something of a psychopath – but a *pure* one. He's quite extraordinary because he is being driven by very destructive forces and yet he has the intelligence and cunning to not reveal everything at once. So he is filled with rage but also with an icy control: all of which makes for a very powerful and dynamic character.'

And it is a character central to the story of *The Hobbit*: 'After Bilbo,' continues Philippa, 'Smaug is the most memorable character in the book. Professor Tolkien had, I think, enormous respect for the origins and mythology of Dragons, depicting them not just as beasts or magical creatures, but also as powerful beings and forces of nature. In the case of Smaug, he not only has massive, earth-shattering, destructive strength, he also commands enormous psychic power: you can't flatter him, lie to him or try to manipulate him. You can't – if you'll excuse the pun – worm your way out of situations with him.'

It's a view shared by Peter: 'No matter how smart you are, Smaug is smarter; he is totally switched on and you can't hope to spin him a line because he's going to see through it straight away. But he is also paranoid. Imagine: he's been sitting there on this gold, luxuriating in it, for two hundred years, knowing one day someone is going to be back, wanting that gold and trying to take it. So he has waited and waited, and when the moment finally comes it's this little creature that doesn't smell like a Dwarf. That's when it's down to Smaug as a paranoid psychopath to get into Bilbo's head and find out why he's there. Who is this intruder and what's his motivation? Is he dangerous? Is he a solitary guy? And, if not, who's behind him? Is there a ten thousand-strong army waiting outside his door? These are the things Smaug has to figure out, and to do so he has to play games.'

It is these aspects to Smaug's character that makes him so appealing, as Philippa explains: 'We see just how much personality Tolkien gives the Dragon in the scene where Bilbo finally confronts Smaug. This is no conventional fairy-tale creature in a children's book: he is sly, deceptive and mesmerizing, seductive but subtle.'

As a writer, Philippa is particularly attracted by one of Tolkien's narrative devices: 'It's interesting that he put his largest creation up against one of his smallest. And yet, there is a sense in which they are equals of sorts. Smaug

OPPOSITE: *The fame of Erebor, and its wealth, would lure the young Dragon down from the north.* ABOVE: *Smaug, the ultimate paranoid psychopath.* BELOW: *Co-Producer & Screenwriter Philippa Boyens with Richard Armitage and Benedict Cumberbatch.*

may not have ever smelt a hobbit before, but he does not make the mistake of underestimating this small creature; far from it. He senses that there's something about this burglar – not just the Ring, but something else as well: perhaps his goodness or his sense of loyalty, and the fact that Bilbo has a strength all his own.'

One way in which that strength manifests itself is in Bilbo's resistance to the lure of gold. Unlike Thorin, he is not susceptible to the envy and greed that, in both book and films, is referred to as 'dragon sickness'. For Smaug, who has lain so long on a hoard of treasure that it is of no use to him beyond his passionate desire for wealth, Bilbo's immunity to gold is perplexing.

For Philippa Boyens, it is the complexities in Bilbo's personality that motivates Smaug's response: 'He quite quickly sets about attempting to undermine the very notions that Bilbo holds onto, which is that he made a promise and is determined to see it through to the finish. Smaug questions Bilbo's commitment. So we have given Smaug a few riddling questions of our own: "What are the risks involved in coming into my lair? Why would the Dwarves send you in here? Do they really care about you? I don't think so! I mean I wouldn't do that to my friend..." These are the kind of tensions we love playing with and building on when we are writing and exploring these ideas. Smaug is, quite simply, a wonderful character and a gift to write for. And, like Gollum, the more you have of him, the more you want!'

TO SEE OR NOT TO SEE

One of Tolkien's original illustrations in *The Hobbit* depicts the encounter between hobbit and Dragon and is titled 'Conversation with Smaug'. In it, Bilbo is shown as a silhouetted figure surrounded by a cloud of mist, indicating that Mr Baggins had taken the precaution of putting on the Ring before venturing into the Dragon's lair. Tolkien's decision to have Smaug conduct a conversation with an invisible Bilbo necessitated a departure from Tolkien's text when it came to filming that scene for *The Desolation of Smaug*. As a result, there comes a point in the exchange when Bilbo removes the Ring and becomes visible.

'I hope the Professor might forgive us for this,' says Philippa, 'but we felt that it was impossible for such a creature not to feel the presence of the Ring. We also knew and understood that, in bringing this scene to life, it would prove difficult to have Bilbo spend the whole time in the shadowy Ring-world effect that we see on screen whenever the hobbit is wearing the Ring, while this other giant creature plays a kind of cat-and-mouse game while searching for him. It became obvious that you could only have an invisible Bilbo for so long before it became unsatisfying and disorientating, that at some point he had to be forced to appear.'

The Forges of Erebor

'The big challenge of the middle film of three,' says Philippa Boyens, 'is finding a way of driving the story to an edge-of-your-seat conclusion where you really, really want to see what happens next and where you have set up everything that you need for the delivery of the third film. So, Peter always knew we had to have a big climax to *The Desolation of Smaug*: we're about to unleash something absolutely terrifying upon the world, and the audience has to understand the full danger of Smaug.'

Tolkien isn't very helpful in addressing such a need because, in the book, Smaug leaves his lair in a rage, destroys the secret door in the mountainside through which the Dwarves entered Erebor, and flies off towards Lake-town without a face-to-face confrontation with Thorin. Early on the filmmakers had reached the decision that such an encounter had to take place, but they had still to work out how it was to happen. Philippa was with Fran Walsh on a flight to Los Angeles, having left Peter thinking about this dilemma. How could Thorin possibly face Smaug when, with some of his companions back in Lake-town, they were no longer even thirteen in number?

'As we talked about it we suddenly said, "What about gold? What about having the Dwarves confront and defeat Smaug by gold? Fighting fire with fire and greed with greed?" Peter took that idea, ran with it and it started to grow. It opened up the whole idea up of the vast wealth of the Dwarves, of the greed of the Dragon, and also the lengths to which both sides – Smaug and Thorin – will go to keep or take possession of the wealth. It showed them both as being equally dangerous in their own way.'

John Howe takes up the story: 'The Dwarves' realization, that the only way to take on something that is a thousand times their size is to use their knowledge of Erebor, leads to a cat-and-mouse pursuit through the Dwarven kingdom involving the mines and industrial-scale foundry that had not previously featured in the films. Peter decided they would light the forges, there would be water cascading and molten gold and all sorts of pitfalls to try to discourage Smaug and generally remain alive.'

OPPOSITE: *Bilbo contemplates how he is going to pull that lever.* ABOVE: *The icy water of the River Running cascades through giant sluices as the Dwarves attempt to drench the Dragon.*

A weekly think-tank came up with ideas for gags and stunts, such as Smaug setting fire to a gallery in one of the coal mines and the Dwarves' various escapades involving buckets on chains, levers and bellows, a great crucible of smelted ore and the casting and releasing of the gigantic – but still molten – statue of Thrór.

Speaking of this climax, Joe Letteri says: 'From a story and character point of view, the idea of topping the sequence off with Smaug looking at that golden statue really tied everything together. The Dragon is in awe because it's gold, but he's also kind of horrified because this thing that he's enthralled to is a statue of a Dwarf – and he hates Dwarves!'

Close-up shots of Bilbo and the Dwarves and some of their action shots were filmed during the 2013 pick-ups, but the environment itself existed only in a growing collection of sketches by Alan Lee and John Howe, as the two concept artists developed visualizations of the various mechanisms required to power and drive the machineries used in the foundry. Every feature was styled to reflect the ornate carved decoration already associated with Dwarvish architecture, such as elaborately detailed waterspouts in the form of huge helmeted Dwarven heads which spew water from their mouths onto the waterwheels set in the stone just below them.

Astonishingly, these settings and the action sequence that unfolds there with hair-raising peril, was accomplished by Weta Digital with breathtaking urgency in the final six weeks leading up to the film's release. 'It wasn't until very late that all those designs got locked together,' recalls Joe, 'and the Forges of Erebor was one of the last sequences that we put through for the film. Pretty much that whole scene was digitally created. You see some close-up shots of the Dwarves but when they're out in the wider forges environment that was all shot on green-screen and everything that you see is digital.'

Indeed, as Joe goes on to reveal, Weta's work wasn't limited to the setting: 'In quite a number of the shots, even the Dwarves are completely digital. If you see them delivering dialogue then they're live-action, but if you see them doing anything else then they're probably digital.'

Reflecting on the developments in technology and the experience gained by Weta Digital in working on such films as *King Kong* and *Avatar*, Joe speaks of enormous changes that have taken place in their technical and artistic abilities: 'Twelve years ago when we were doing a character like Gollum, we were just trying to understand what it is that makes a character, or a person in the real world, both appear to be alive and also engaging when you see them up on the screen.

We were really approaching it from the outside-in at that point, because we had so little time to study the problem, so it was really a lot of work that was being handcrafted. In the years since then the science has evolved. What we've really tried to do is study, and understand, and quantify what these things are that we're trying to achieve. Probably for the viewer it's a subtle difference, but it lends a level of realism that allows you to sink into what you're seeing on the screen just a little bit more.'

The effectiveness with which Bilbo, Thorin and the Dwarves' heart-in-mouth encounter with Smaug unfolds in the mines and forges of Erebor would seem to prove the point.

THE FORGES OF EREBOR

THE VOICE OF SMAUG

'Smaug needed a great voice,' says Peter Jackson, 'and Benedict Cumberbatch gave it to us.' Now known for his starring roles in *War Horse*, *Star Trek Into Darkness* and *12 Years a Slave*, Benedict had come to the attention of the screen-writers of *The Hobbit* through his hit BBC television series, *Sherlock*.

Benedict was not, however, the only actor in the running for the voice of the Dragon. 'We met with some great performers with great voices,' recalls Peter, 'but when we met Benedict in London we discovered that, apart from the voice (and it *is* a wonderful voice), he had been a huge fan of *The Hobbit* from childhood and really understood Smaug's character.'

There was an immediate rapport between the team from Wellington and the London-born actor: 'Quite simply, Benedict understood Smaug as well as we did! We had spent a long time figuring out how we wanted the Dragon to be played and when Benedict walked in and read the script, it was obvious that he abso-lutely *knew* Smaug and how to play him. He had all the charm together with – just beneath the surface – that edgy tension that makes him so unpredictable and dangerous.'

This synchronicity was all it took for Smaug to get his voice. 'At that point,' says Peter, 'we immediately knew that our Dragon was in safe hands. If you've got an intelligent actor with a fantastic voice, who also knows *The Hobbit* and loves everything that Smaug thinks and does, then you've got three things which can come together to create a perfect storm.'

PETER JACKSON ON BARD

For a filmmaker, the character of Bard – in terms of Tolkien's book – is a significantly underdeveloped character, since the author gives only the barest essentials necessary to establish him as Bard the Bowman, the champion archer who takes on Smaug when the Dragon turns his wrath against Lake-town. Peter Jackson explains how he and his fellow screenwriters tackled this problem:

'In the films we really wanted to have Bard's storyline be one that organically carries on after his confrontation with the Dragon, so his primary focus becomes the welfare of his people. The former rogue black-market trader naturally assumes a leadership role and people who were once Bard's enemies, like the Master's guards, now declare loyalty to him. Even though this results in his having quite an effective fighting force at his command, his first and foremost interest is simply to feed, clothe, and house his people. As a result, Bard has some of the purest motives of any character in this film, although he and the folk from Lake-town are eventually and inevitably drawn into the Battle of the Five Armies.

'Luke Evans gives a tremendous performance as Bard and in *The Battle of the Five Armies* you see Bard's character grow and develop, from the man we have already got to know as a father to his family, into someone who becomes the father figure to everybody in Lake-town.'

OPPOSITE: *With bow in hand, Bard is ready for action.* THIS PAGE, TOP TO BOTTOM: *Luke Evans must be feeling the heat as he is without Bard's coat, but fortunately plenty of fire extinguishers stand ready in case things get too hot to handle; Bard is dressed for battle as he receives instruction from his director; on set among the Dale ruins with Ian McKellen.*

SMAUG THE MIGHTY & THE DARK LORD

Unbeknownst to Bilbo when he wrote up the account of his expedition to the Lonely Mountain in *The Red Book of Westmarch* (from which are derived, in Tolkien's imaginary realm, the narratives of *The Hobbit* and *The Lord of the Rings*), greater dramas were unfolding across Middle-earth. Much of this detail is chronicled in the author's Appendices to *The Lord of the Rings* (which have helped shape the writing of the screenplays for *The Hobbit*) and in an unfinished and posthumously published fragment entitled 'The Quest of Erebor', which can be found in Tolkien's *Unfinished Tales*.

It becomes clear from reading these sources that Gandalf had long been anxious about Smaug beyond his theft of the Dwarves' home and wealth, concerned that an alliance might be formed between Sauron and the creature. 'The Dragon of Erebor is on my mind,' the Wizard says at one point, and, years after the event, reflects: 'Sauron... was preparing for a great war... The Dragon Sauron might use with terrible effect. How then could the end of Smaug be achieved?' The answer, perhaps, was through the Dwarves' desire for revenge – aided by the wits of a hobbit burglar...

Luke Evans
BARD THE BOWMAN

'HE IS SORT OF THE ARAGORN OF *THE HOBBIT*.' LUKE EVANS IS RECALLING HOW HIS CHARACTER, BARD, WAS FIRST INTRODUCED TO HIM BY THE FILMMAKERS AND THERE ARE, INDEED, SIMILARITIES: BOTH ARE MEN WHO HAVE TO PROVE THEMSELVES BEFORE FULFILLING THEIR DESTINIES. THEY ARE ALSO BOTH HUMANS IN A REALM PEOPLED BY MANY RACES, CREATURES AND BEINGS: 'MIDDLE-EARTH IS FULL OF HOBBITS, DWARVES, ELVES, ORCS AND WIZARDS,' NOTES LUKE, 'AND BEING ONE OF THE ONLY HUMANS IN THE FILM I FELT A SENSE OF RESPONSIBILITY BECAUSE I FELT THAT, THROUGH MY EYES, THE HUMAN AUDIENCE MIGHT BE ABLE TO VIEW MIDDLE-EARTH, AND ALSO BE ABLE TO UNDERSTAND AND BE SYMPATHETIC TO MY CHARACTER, BECAUSE HE IS GOING THROUGH HUMAN EMOTIONS.'

Although audiences did not meet Bard until the second film of the trilogy, he was quickly established as a character of both immediate and continuing importance within the story of *The Hobbit*. In discussing his role, Luke references his own favourite film genre: 'I love watching movies with action heroes and superheroes, particularly those with a vulnerable side to them where you can see some of the cracks in the image and watch them fight through those difficulties to become the heroic leader. Bard is, essentially, that character – someone who, when you first meet him in the film, the last thing you would ever think is that this is a guy capable of heroic deeds or of having great leadership potential when it comes to tackling the wicked, dark forces of the world.'

Exploring that development of Bard's character, Luke says: 'At the beginning of *The Desolation of Smaug*, when you first see him in Lake-town, Bard is a lowly bargeman desperately trying to earn a living and raise three children on his own.' Laughing, Luke adds, 'Originally in the script Bard was going to have a dog as well, but the screenwriters got rid of it: I think they realized that would have been a nightmare. I mean, come on! He's a bargeman! Three kids *and* a dog? That's another mouth to feed!'

Luke's comment reflects the nature of life in Lake-town: 'They are living hand-to-mouth in this town that's little more than a controlled state where nobody has any aspirations beyond survival. Bard simply wants to keep his children alive and safe and will do whatever it takes to protect them. If there's a problem and he can sort it without there being any bloodshed, that's what he'll do.'

OPPOSITE: *Luke Evans as Bard, carrying the sword of his ancestor, Girion.* ABOVE: *Bard strides purposefully away from an unsuccessful conversation with Thorin outside the Front Gate of Erebor.*

However, as Luke explains, when Bard and his family get caught up in the fate of Thorin's Company of Dwarves the situation changes: 'Initially, he realizes he can make a little bit of money from the Dwarves by smuggling them into Lake-town, but I don't believe he thinks much further than that or even begins to see that the Dwarves have their own agenda. But once in Lake-town, he finds that there's more to them than meets the eye.'

This relationship, that plays out to dramatic consequences in *The Battle of the Five Armies*, begins with mutual distrust: 'The Dwarves adopt a bad attitude towards Bard, especially Thorin, who has a very bombastic manner about him and it is clear that he and Dwalin don't like this bargeman. Bard helps them out, does what he can, but it's not enough for Thorin and they are not grateful; so my response is: "Well, I'm doing you a favour, but I'm not putting my life – or that of my kids – in danger!"'

That danger is the single-minded determination of Thorin and Company to recover their ancestral home; a Quest, if they succeed, that will inevitably awaken the

♦ *There are various ways to draw a bow, depending on its size but this bow was so large and the arrows were so long that I had to invert my fingers just to pull the bowstring past my face in order to give it enough length and leverage* ♦

Dragon Smaug, the sleeping but ever-present danger beneath the Lonely Mountain. Bard knows his history and is well aware of the Dragon's devastating power.

'When Smaug came to take Erebor,' says Luke, 'he attacked the city of Dale and Bard's ancestor, Lord Girion, who was a mighty archer, bravely but unsuccessfully fought to defend his people with bow and arrow. In Bard's memory is the recollection of just how dangerous this Dragon is, and of the devastation, pain and death that followed.'

Bard's fears are fully justified when Smaug's rage at Thorin's return brings the Dragon out of his lair, for it is Lake-town that faces the full impact of his wrath. That is when Bard the Bargeman becomes Bard the Bowman…

In preparation for the role, Luke needed to master the skills of archery, as he explains: 'I did a lot of training with the bow although, as it turned out, the training was not much help beyond getting the feel for handling the weapon, because the longbow that I finally use in the film was actually taller than me! There are various ways to draw a bow, depending on its size, but this bow was so large and the arrows were so long that I had to invert my

fingers just to pull the bowstring past my face in order to give it enough length and leverage.'

Luke recalls his first day's filming on *The Hobbit*, when Bard is forced to confront the fiery onslaught of the Dragon: 'Hour after hour, I'd been scrambling around across the icy roofs of Lake-town and then they add real fire, hand me this six-foot bow and a quiver with arrows the size of my leg and tell me to run from a Dragon that I can't see! And we proceeded to do that for almost fifteen hours!'

On getting the part of the Lake-town hero, Luke had told Peter Jackson that he wanted to do as many of his own stunts as possible, and after a week's training that's exactly what he found himself doing. 'By the end of that first day, my hands were skinned and shredded – from my knuckles down, they were blood red! But I'd got through it, and I honestly think Pete was testing me, seeing how far he could push me, his way of saying, "All right, if you want to do this and run these rooftops, be my guest!" So I did – for three or four days!'

Luke is quick to point out that he was hitched to a cable and that the Lake-town set had been partially rebuilt in a studio so that it was just the roofs rather than the entire buildings. 'That was a good thing because it meant that if I'd fallen it wouldn't have been more than about thirty feet, which was not so bad and certainly better than seventy feet or more! I can't imagine what's it's going to be like to watch those scenes, because it'll bring back all the pain, the heat, the exhaustion; but also, of course, the satisfaction of getting through what was a really great experience.'

There was also, he reveals, an added benefit to having an outsize bow: 'I actually used it for more than just shooting arrows – during one scene I utilized it to help pull myself up onto one of the rooftops. That's Bard for you: he's very practical – he'll use whatever he's got.'

As Smaug descends on Lake-town, Bard is the one person who may be able to defeat the Dragon and save his people. All he has to rely on, however, is his innate courage; the help of his son, Bain; his memories of the story of his ancestor, Girion – and a single Black Arrow.

OPPOSITE, CLOCKWISE FROM TOP LEFT: *Luke Evans waits for the Dwarves to arrive while filming on the Pelorus River; Bard encounters the Elven soldiers of Mirkwood; Luke Evans' first day on set was an eventful one; among the ruins of Dale; sharing a joke with John Bell; Bard the Bowman in action.*

THE BLACK ARROW

ANYONE HOPING TO KILL A DRAGON AS HUGE AND POWERFUL AS SMAUG WOULD NEED A VERY PARTICULAR WEAPON, AND FOR BARD THE BOWMAN THERE IS ONLY ONE SUCH POSSIBILITY: THE BLACK ARROW. IT IS THE LAST OF A NUMBER OF ARROWS SAID TO HAVE BEEN FORGED BENEATH THE LONELY MOUNTAIN AND GIVEN BY THORIN'S GRANDFATHER, THRÓR, TO BARD'S ANCESTOR, LORD GIRION. GIRION USED ALL BUT ONE IN THE UNSUCCESSFUL DEFENCE OF DALE WHEN SMAUG ATTACKED THE CITY PRIOR TO DRIVING THE DWARVES OUT OF EREBOR.

Designing a weapon with Dragon-slaying potential was as crucial as designing a Dragon, as Weta Workshop's Richard Taylor remembers: 'Although Peter didn't necessarily know exactly what he was after, he knew that what he didn't want was a boring, standard arrowhead.'

'Over a period of a few weeks,' recalls John Howe, 'I was scribbling in my diary as many different kinds of curious and unusual arrowheads as I could imagine and eventually Peter chose one with a weird twisty-headed design.'

As the person charged with turning John's drawing into a physical object, Richard Taylor gives a more technical description of the weapon: 'The idea, after many rounds of design, was for an arrowhead shaped like an open corkscrew with two tangs that, in theory, would rotate through the target's body, taking out a fairly sizeable core-sample of the creature's flesh.' As Richard goes on to explain, it proved a surprisingly difficult object to make: 'The Black Arrow was a comprehensive manufacturing challenge. To anyone watching the movie it looks so simple: a rod with some feathers and a steel end. But it has to be built so that it can be lightweight and durable, but not flexible. Not only that, but for reasons of safety on set we had to be sure that if anyone – other than a Dragon – were to be jabbed by it they wouldn't be injured.'

The other key sticking point, as it were, in relation to this, which will be answered in the final part of the trilogy, is having made such an arrow, how would you fire it…?

ABOVE: *Black Arrows were kept in Dale's armoury and fired from giant wind lances.* RIGHT: *As the descendant of Girion, Lord of Dale, Bard possesses the last Black Arrow.*

EYEBALL TO TENNIS BALL

Acting is hard work when your director asks you to imagine you are looking up into the sky and seeing an enormous Dragon flying overhead, as John Bell found when he was filming scenes as Bard's son, Bain, during Smaug's attack on Lake-town. 'My Smaug,' he laughs, 'was a tennis ball with an angry face drawn on it stuck on the end of a stick!'

Peter Jackson did, however, make a few helpful suggestions on how to visualize the Dragon: 'Peter gave me an idea of Smaug's size, telling me to think him as being about the size of an Airbus A380 – the world's largest passenger airliner – which is something pretty big! After that, I just used my imagination a lot: picturing him red and scaly and looking down on me with his cat-like eyes.'

TOP: *Bard and Bain look over the top of the camera at what's approaching.* ABOVE: *Richard Armitage and Lee Pace were each filmed separately, with 'tennis balls' to guide their eye line, so that the on-screen confrontation between Thorin and Thranduil could be composited together convincingly.*

SOUNDS FANTASTIC

FILM IS SO VISUAL A MEDIUM THAT WE ARE OFTEN UNCONSCIOUS OF JUST HOW IMPORTANT ARE THE SOUNDS WE HEAR WHEN WE ARE SEEING. THE WORLD OF THE MOVIE SOUND BOFFIN MAY NOT BE AS GLAMOROUS AS MANY OF THE OTHER JOBS IN FILMMAKING, BUT IT REQUIRES A LIVELY – EVEN QUIRKY – INVENTIVENESS THAT ALLOWS YOU TO HEAR OFTEN ORDINARY AND EVERYDAY SOUNDS AND IMAGINE HOW THEY COULD BE MADE BY SOMETHING OUTLANDISH AND FANTASTICAL – SUCH AS THE EXTRAORDINARY CREATURES ENCOUNTERED IN MIDDLE-EARTH.

Elsewhere in this book, you can read about how these audio wizards set about creating the sounds of battles, but here are one or two insights into some of their other idiosyncratic solutions to such questions as…

What do giant spiders sound like? **David Farmer, Sound Designer:** 'When the spiders were just milling about their nest, their vocals were made up of dolphin and killer whale clicks that gave them a lot of nice communication from the natural animal world while also having a very insect-like "hive" quality. When they started fighting the Dwarves, their vocals changed into screams and hisses. The screams were largely made of killer whale squeals and the hisses were made from mountain lions, tigers, snakes and badgers. The concept was that when Bilbo put on the Ring all of the creature sounds turned into words that Bilbo could understand. The actors' voices were then vocoded with some white noise to give them a more hissy, flattened character, and then clicks that had been performed by one of the actors were overlaid against the dialogue to carefully follow the shape of the words.'

What sound does a spider-web have? **Justin Doyle, Assistant Sound Effects Editor:** 'We'd decided the webs should be dry sounding, not too wet and gooey. They also needed some tensile strength to both restrain and suspend the cocooned Dwarves. We recorded a wide range of materials to see what various things sounded like and how the different combinations of sounds would work together. We shrink-wrapped bundles of bark, leaves, flax and charcoal and pressed and stretched and pulled on those. We also recorded every kind of sticky tape we could find and peeled it off plenty of different surfaces. Combinations of those sounds gave us the texture and the stretch of the webs. The tearing of the webs was more difficult as it had to be larger and stronger than the other sounds. Our assistant editor, Rowan Watson, had recorded some kelp seaweed for the fish pouring from the barrels in Lake-town and he happened to tear up some large pieces when he had finished, which was just the sound of big, fibrous and slightly fleshy tears we were after.'

How do you create the sound of a man who turns into a bear? **Sound Designer Dave Whitehead says they started with the obvious:** 'I recorded a grizzly bear in Canada and David Farmer recorded one in the USA. It seemed the logical way to go for Beorn the skin-changer. But once we were in the mix, Peter decided that he would like something other than bear sounds, something that was almost Jurassic. So, the final vocals for Beorn are a complete mix of sounds: there are still a few bear breaths and roars in there, but the main source is an unlikely combination of elephants and a squeaky oven door!'

OPPOSITE, TOP TO BOTTOM: *The Ring makes its presence felt in Mirkwood forest; the sound of an attacking spider was comprised of a menagerie of exotic animals; Beorn the man is a normal host but once in bear-form he would be voiced by far more unexpected sources!*

FIRE & WATER

One of the chapters in J.R.R. Tolkien's *The Hobbit* is entitled 'Fire and Water' and these elements – along with earth and air – have significant symbolic importance in all Tolkien's books, strengthening the mythological nature of his writing.

When it comes to filmmaking, however, they are curiously elusive sounds to successfully capture and replicate. Here, Sound Designers, Dave Whitehead and David Farmer, reveal how they and their colleagues helped create the sounds of fire and water…

'The first thing you learn,' says Dave Whitehead, 'is that, if you are not very careful, you can easily melt the precious fluffy wind protectors on your microphones! I've done this twice: the first time while recording the furnace on a steam engine and again by getting too close to a huge bonfire. Lots of crew recorded their fireplaces and braziers for smaller fires and I bought some 'fire pois', which are basically a big wick on a chain that you soak in kerosene, set on fire and spin around. These are particularly good for creating fire *whoosh*es and similar effects – but need careful handling!'

In the very specific case of Dragon fire, David Farmer explains that Smaug's inflammable exhalations required something special to add power and movement: 'While there are elements of torch *whoosh*es in Smaug's fiery breath, they only play a minor role in the overall effect, which combines a lot of different sounds to give the fire an emotive presence that's a bit more interesting than real fire could ever sound. Dragon fire is mainly made up of various animal growls, mixed with rocket launches and, for additional crunch, some hyped-up recordings of piles of tree branches with one or two ice-cracks to give extra punch. The sound of Smaug drawing in a lungful of air before breathing out his fireball is a recording of me making strained inhaling sounds. To heighten the threat of danger and give the fireballs a physical component that real fire doesn't have, we added the sound of a heavy impact whenever a fireball hit an object.'

Water, as Dave Whitehead explains, presents a different set of challenges: 'Any large mass of water – like a fast-running river or a waterfall – simply sounds like a wall of white noise. Some of the most useful water sounds actually come from unusual sources. We had access to the wet set for Lake-town, so we put on waders and recorded all kinds of water-related sounds: bubbles and splashes, boats bobbing and wooden, plastic and cardboard barrels hitting the water. The main sound source for the barrels travelling downriver used a treated recording of a very large fishing sinker attached to a very thick piece of nylon and dragged along at speed, which gave a swift movement like it was ripping through the water.'

THORIN & BILBO

'**I**F YOU DON'T STAY ON TOP THINGS,' SAYS PHILIPPA BOYENS, 'YOU CAN FIND YOURSELF WITH A LEAD CHARACTER WHO ALL HE EVER DOES IS REACT TO WHAT EVERYBODY ELSE IS DOING OR SAYING.' WITH A LAUGH, SHE ADDS: 'SUDDENLY YOU REALIZE THAT EVERYTHING YOU'VE WRITTEN IS SOME VARIATION ON "CLOSE-UP OF THORIN LOOKING GRIM...", "THORIN LOOKING STERN..." OR "THORIN LOOKING TROUBLED..."'

It is a well-known fact that many actors would rather play a 'character role' than the hero or heroine, as Philippa notes: 'It can often be far more satisfying for an actor to play some interesting secondary character than the lead because it's possible to be more extreme, more colourful. And, in a funny kind of way, those characters are often the ones who drive the storytelling.'

In the case of Thorin, the challenge facing the screenwriters was to make him more than just a serious, grim-faced warrior: 'True, he's carrying a lot on his shoulders, but that can't be his whole story. The audience needs to have an understanding of his desires and anxieties; they need to feel a sense of his vulnerability. One of the most interesting ways in which we did that was in our depiction of the relationship between Thorin and Bilbo.'

Summing up that relationship, Philippa says: 'Thorin finds Bilbo an incredibly irksome burden and yet he doesn't hesitate, when necessary, to jump down a cliff and pull him to safety. That's just who Thorin is. It's innate. By the end of the first film, you saw the trust that has developed between these two characters: a bond of friendship that unites this mighty Dwarf warrior, this grizzled person who's endured a lot of hardship, with the slightly lonely, eccentric character of Bilbo who's also full of hobbit goodness and decency and down-to-earth common sense. That trust and acceptance was maintained through the second film until, towards the end, when we introduce an element that becomes incredibly important in the third film and which will be the ultimate test of that relationship...'

RIGHT: *Bilbo and Thorin stand together in Mirkwood forest to face whatever is next about to confront them.*

Victoria Sullivan,
Script Supervisor & Continuity

KEEPING EVERYONE ON THE SAME PAGE

'**I** AM THE ONLY PERSON IN MY DEPARTMENT, AND I WORK WITH ALL THE DEPARTMENTS ON SET.' VICTORIA SULLIVAN DOES ONE OF THE MOST UNDER-RATED AND YET TOTALLY ESSENTIAL JOBS ON *THE HOBBIT*, THAT OF SCRIPT SUPERVISOR AND CONTINUITY. 'IN FACT,' SHE GOES ON, 'I CAN'T THINK OF ANY DEPARTMENT THAT I DON'T HAVE SOMETHING TO DO WITH. MY JOB IS REALLY THE CENTRE OF THE WHEEL, THE POINT AT WHICH ALL THE DEPARTMENTS WITH THEIR INDIVIDUAL SKILLS AND RESPONSIBILITIES MEET, AND IT'S PART OF MY TASK TO MAKE SURE THEY'RE ALL ON THE SAME SCENE ON THE SAME PAGE AT THE SAME TIME.'

Every day on *The Hobbit* trilogy and, before that, *The Lord of the Rings* and *King Kong*, Victoria Sullivan could be found alongside director, Peter Jackson, and editor, Jabez Olssen, keeping careful records – Victoria refers to them as 'squiggly lines in books' – of every shot in the script. These records form the basis of the complex, detailed process of logging every individual take of every single shot of the hundreds and thousands in the entire film.

Of the other part of her job, Victoria says: 'Being in charge of continuity means I am the editor's eyes and ears on set.'

There's nothing more that film buffs love than spotting

inconsistencies in continuity: those little mistakes – sometimes glaring errors – that break the filmmaking illusion and stop the suspension of disbelief: from a suddenly appearing or disappearing prop to an unexplained change in an item of costume between one shot and the next. Victoria Sullivan's job is to try and prevent such mishaps: 'Some people think continuity's about checking the props, wardrobe and make-up and it is, but it's also about keeping an eye on the detail of the cuts. I have to ensure that each actor repeats their actions: that they sit down or pick something up on the same line in every take so that the various takes can be seamlessly cut together later.'

Summing up her responsibility for continuity, Victoria says: 'Essentially, continuity is a bit like choreography: it's got a flow to it, and it's all got to fit together in an end result, even though we shoot the film as a jigsaw puzzle. Providing I look after the details and communicate with the other departments correctly, we have everything ready so that Peter can get on with directing the drama and dealing with the actors without being bothered with the often small, but always necessary, details, that will eventually help put the whole film together.'

OPOSITE, LEFT TO RIGHT: *Peter reviews the latest script changes with Ryan Gage, Ian McKellen & Martin Freeman; Balin checks that everything is in order.* ABOVE: *Victoria Sullivan keeps a close eye on continuity in 3D.* BELOW: *Sitting in front of their monitors in the snow-covered desolation of Dale, Peter and Victoria Sullivan prepare to keep a close eye on the next scene.*

KEEPING EVERYONE ON THE SAME PAGE

WHY MARTIN FREEMAN *is* BILBO

'I AM JUST SO HAPPY THAT MARTIN FREEMAN ENDED UP IN THIS MOVIE,' SAYS PETER JACKSON OF HIS LEADING ACTOR – MAN AND HOBBIT. 'I'M SITTING IN THE CUTTING ROOM, PUTTING TOGETHER THE THIRD AND FINAL FILM AND THINKING, "GOD, MARTIN IS SUCH A TERRIFIC ACTOR!" HE'S SO BRILLIANT FOR THIS ROLE, BECAUSE HE'S CONSTANTLY EXPLORING AND EXPERIMENTING; EVERY TAKE IS DIFFERENT, GIVING ME WONDERFULLY ENTERTAINING CHOICES SO I CAN EDIT TOGETHER THE FILM IN SEVERAL DIFFERENT WAYS. I WATCH WHAT HE DOES WITH GENUINE ASTONISHMENT: SIX OR SEVEN TAKES AND NEVER THE SAME. YOU ASK YOURSELF, HOW MANY DIFFERENT WAYS CAN YOU SAY A LINE AND KEEP IT ALWAYS ENTERTAINING, SOMETIMES AMUSING, BUT ALWAYS TRUTHFUL?'

In particular, Peter praises the way in which Martin Freeman's performance as Bilbo has captured the development of the character: 'He's really managed to make Bilbo grow and mature across these three films. You never feel with Martin's portrayal that he's settled into a predictable pattern, he's constantly getting himself deeper into the character. By the third film, Bilbo has gained a lot of self confidence and a certain level of worldliness. But the most testing time still lies ahead for him as he attempts to deal with Thorin's growing madness and as he faces a major moral dilemma in seeking to prevent the battle.'

'Sometimes,' says Philippa Boyens, 'after you've been working with an actor for a while and you start seeing the rushes, you begin to look at them and think to yourself, "I cannot imagine anybody else ever having played this character." The weird thing with Martin Freeman was, we already knew that *before* we started filming.'

Recalling that time, Philippa explains: 'It had been in the back of our minds for a very long time that, if we ever did *The Hobbit*, Martin *was* the hobbit. Bilbo is a difficult character to play; Martin makes it look deceptively easy,

but you need an actor with a great range who can play not just the comedy but, in a very real way, the drama. He can be vulnerable at the same time as being staunch and strong; he can be funny at the same time as having great pathos.'

There were also certain athletic requirements: 'Bilbo is forever climbing up trees, fighting Goblins, falling down places, hanging off the edge of cliffs and things like that. Not only was Martin able to do those things, but above everything else he had that essential quality of being immediately likeable to an audience.'

Summing up her assessment, Philippa says: '*The Hobbit* is not the story of someone setting out to save the world. Bilbo's adventure is the tale of a slightly eccentric hobbit who's finally decided to tumble out his door and follow this rowdy bunch of Dwarves on a treasure hunt. Of course, there's much more to it than that in the end, but that's how it starts and the great thing about Martin Freeman is that he takes you on that journey with him and shows us how Bilbo changes and why that change is so entirely for the better.'

Martin is such a terrific actor!" He's so brilliant for this role, because he's constantly exploring and experimenting; every take is different, giving me wonderfully entertaining choices

THIS PAGE: *By the time of the Battle of the Five Armies, Bilbo is a very different hobbit to the one who started this journey.* OVERLEAF: *The many faces of Bilbo Baggins, thanks to the brilliant performance of Martin Freeman.*

Cate Blanchett
GALADRIEL

'I WAS A STALKER!' SAYS CATE BLANCHETT. 'AS SOON AS I HEARD PETER JACKSON WAS GOING TO EMBARK UPON *THE HOBBIT*, I WAS CALLING MY AGENT PRETTY MUCH EVERY DAY TO SAY, "IS THERE ANY WORD YET? IS GALADRIEL GOING TO BE IN IT?" AND I KEPT GETTING THE ANSWER, "PETER DOESN'T KNOW YET." UNDERSTANDABLY, OF COURSE, BECAUSE GALADRIEL DOESN'T APPEAR IN THE BOOK, BUT I JUST KEPT HOPING AGAINST HOPE. FRANKLY, I WOULD HAVE DONE ANYTHING – I'D HAVE SERVED DRINKS IN THE BACKGROUND – SO, WHEN I FINALLY GOT WORD THAT GALADRIEL WOULD BE IN THE FILMS, I WAS OVER THE MOON!'

For Cate there were many happy recollections of previously working with Peter: 'He was the reason that I was so excited about being part *The Lord of the Rings* trilogy – and, of course, Galadriel was just a teeny-weenie piece of what is such an extraordinary puzzle. And I really don't think anyone other than Peter could have ever put it all together, because he's got an astonishing sense of the sublimely beautiful and the strangely grotesque and combines those two elements in an utterly unique way.'

One reason she was so keen to get back to the realm of hobbits, Elves and Wizards was because, since appearing in *The Lord of the Rings*, Cate and her husband, Andrew Upton, had started a family. 'I wanted to be part of this,' Cate explains, 'so that my children could see it and I returned to Wellington's Stone Street Studios with my three boys. I felt it was a real gift for them to be able to be there and witness the expertise and the genius behind the film.'

So how did her sons react? Cate laughs: 'For them, it's a case of: forget all my other work in theatre or on film, *this* is the only thing that I've ever done!'

Like the other returning *Rings* cast-members, it was a very particular experience: 'It was a little bit like going back to summer camp: finding that so many of the people who were part of the first journey, begun twelve years ago, were now part of this journey. Head of Make-up and Hair, Peter Swords King, pulled out Galadriel's wig and it was like seeing some kind of curious creature emerge. I know

it sounds rather clichéd, but as soon as I put on that wig, the whole thing felt timeless.'

There was also the excitement of some stunning new costumes created by Ann Maskrey: 'They were really beautiful; a lot of the fabrics were from India and the beadwork was exquisite. The attention to detail was exceptional: take the dress Galadriel wears at the meeting of the White Council in Rivendell, there were thousands of sequins – not on top, which would have been garish, but on the second layer of the garment so that there was a sheen and a sparkle that was almost as if light was radiating out of the costume.'

Not that this beautiful gown was without its challenges, as Cate admits: 'The dress had a really long train and when I first put it on I said to Peter, "I hope there aren't any plans for me to walk in this?" Fortunately there weren't and Peter had the steps built specially for that wonderful *Ziegfeld Follies* moment when Gandalf sees Galadriel for the first time.'

Recalling the scene where Galadriel debates the Quest of Erebor with Gandalf, Elrond and Saruman, Cate says: 'There is a hot-headedness about Elrond that is quite different to Galadriel's temperament. She is much more measured and always able to temper what she senses is coming with what she's experiencing. She is also the consummate listener. A lot of what goes on in the White Council scene is her weighing up what other people are thinking.'

The actor also reveals that a fair amount of behind-the-scenes fun went on: 'Hugo Weaving and Ian McKellen

darkness that no one else is prepared to enter.'

There is a comment made by Gandalf to Galadriel when the two are left alone at the end of the White Council that Cate finds especially poignant. Asked why he chose to send Bilbo on the Quest, the Wizard remarks, 'Saruman believes that it is only great power that can hold evil in check, but that is not what I have found. I've found it is the small things – everyday deeds of ordinary folk – that keep the darkness at bay, simple acts of kindness and love. Why Bilbo Baggins? Perhaps it is because I am afraid, and he gives me courage.'

'In Ian's performance,' says Cate, 'there's not a trace of sentiment but what he says about the small people, and the insignificant things, is so moving. And if you took just that speech alone and then went and watched *The Lord of the Rings*, it has such a beautiful resonance with Gandalf's relationship with Frodo.'

This awareness of a future that has yet to be played out is something of which Cate is very conscious: the fact that audiences watching *The Hobbit* are simultaneously seeing events unfold while realizing that those events will inevitably lead to the fracturing of the White Council, the treachery of Saruman and the rise of Sauron. 'Having the memory of the other films,' she says, 'gives *The Hobbit* a very particular resonance that sets off some really interesting vibrations. In a way it's a gift that it has been filmed second, with this prescience of what is to come.'

Cate speaks of the enigmatic moment in the Rivendell Council Chamber when Galadriel is there and then, a moment later, gone. 'I was just interested in the idea that, perhaps, Gandalf has a sense memory of her, so Galadriel could just appear and disappear.' She pauses, laughs and then adds, 'Since Peter gave me such a glorious *Ziegfeld Follies*-style entrance, I thought, why not have a lovely exit!'

When they part in *An Unexpected Journey*, Galadriel makes Gandalf a promise: 'If you should ever need my help, I will come.' She fulfils that promise in *The Battle*

are both rather wicked men and I quite enjoy a little bit of wickedness. So there were times when it was rather like being at the back of the school bus. Hugo had nicknames for us: he was Elrondo, Gandalf was Gandy and I was Gladys. Of course, everyone on set loves a giggle and, especially when you're doing scenes that are portentous, it's really important to keep it alive and buoyant and this sort of naughtiness can actually help.'

Asked about the relationship between Galadriel and Gandalf, that in *The Hobbit: An Unexpected Journey* is portrayed as being warmly affectionate, Cate responds: 'Well, for starters, it's not hard to be flirtatious with Ian. And it was important to make their relationship as dynamic as possible. After all, who knows, perhaps in another life… There might even be a further movie for Peter: *The Secret Life of Gladys and Gandy*!'

From Tolkien's writings we learn that The White Council was formed at the request of Galadriel and, on a serious note, Cate adds: 'I see her and Gandalf as kindred spirits who have a similar perspective on events – the perspective of outsiders. They have a suspicion that something terrible is coming, a sense of foreboding that something is deeply wrong in this place that seems to be at peace. There are things afoot, fissures in the spirit of Middle-earth and what is truly noble and heroic about Gandalf and Galadriel is that they are prepared, together, to look evil in the eye. That's what makes Gandalf such a wonderful hero for our own age. To have the courage to go against popular opinion and to move on into the *of the Five Armies* when, at Dol Guldur, the Wizard confronts the Necromancer. As in *The Fellowship of the Ring*, the filmmakers opted to explore, once more, a surprising aspect to Galadriel's character. 'It is almost,' says Cate, 'as if you cannot have good without the threat of it being challenged and even taken over to the dark side, as if you can only know shadow when you know light. Peter wanted to give a shadow to Galadriel in *The Lord of the Rings*, and he really went there in *The Hobbit*. He referred to it as "psychic distress", that sense of a war within, that internal battle between one's dark side and one's better self. In coming to Gandalf's aid, Galadriel has to grapple with the seductive power of the Necromancer to draw other beings into a void of darkness, despair and decay. She has to summon every particle of her strength to resist and, in doing so, we see Galadriel's incredible power and realize that – but for the fineness and strength of her spirit – how quickly that power for goodness could be turned to evil.'

An astonishing moment in Galadriel's struggle with the Necromancer is when she uses the language of the enemy. 'Unlike Elvish,' says Cate, 'Black Speech is thick, harsh and very guttural. It's completely unexpected and shocking that such a sound would ever emerge from her mouth. I hear Benedict Cumberbatch can say it *backwards*. I find that absolutely gob-smacking: "The Academy Award for Backwards Black Speech goes to——" *Astonishing!*'

Because Ian McKellen wasn't available for all the scenes shot at Dol Guldur, he had a dummy understudy. 'We called it "Michael" because Ian and I thought it looked a bit like Michael Gambon. We shot some footage with the dummy before Ian had a chance to do any. I think it was a bit of a low moment for Ian when I told him that he would have to try and match what the dummy had already done. It was a bit cheeky, but he did it very gracefully and, in the end, he did it better,' Cate laughs; 'well, marginally.'

For Cate Blanchett, the last day of filming her scenes was one that she didn't want to come and, when it did, she was reluctant to accept the fact, thinking that she might, perhaps, be able to make it back for a final fleeting appearance on the final day of shooting. 'I didn't want to let go,' she recalls, 'so I told Peter that I was still stalking him! And, having seen all the Dwarf beards and fallen in love with them and heard that there was going to be a banqueting scene, I said, "I want to come back and be a Dwarf, I want to wear one of those beards and you and I can sit there, just in a passing shot, eating a chicken leg."

Unfortunately that quirky ambition was unrealized because Cate and her husband's commitments to the Sydney Theatre Company didn't permit her return to Wellington. The actor continues, however, 'hoping against hope', as she explains: 'I still keep thinking that, maybe, there'll be some sort of last-minute re-shoot so I can squeeze every last drop out of the experience and have Galadriel walk through the back of battle.'

No one has better captured the essence of the mysterious and beautiful Elvish nature than Cate Blanchett: 'They are,' she says, 'a race apart, a highly evolved species with a deep understanding of the power of peace that a lot of other races in Middle-earth don't comprehend. Being Elven is an interesting challenge because it's about finding fluidity and grace – while, in my case, walking in disco platform boots because Elves are very tall and I think I always needed the height! Depending on the shot, of course: I didn't have to wear them as much in scenes with Ian, but then Wizards are tall – maybe that's the attraction between Gladys and Gandy: they're both the right height!'

Alan Lee & John Howe
SHARED VISION

ALAN LEE AND JOHN HOWE HAVE SPENT THE BETTER PART OF SEVENTEEN YEARS WORKING TOGETHER AS CONCEPT ARTISTS ON, FIRST, *THE LORD OF THE RINGS* AND THEN *THE HOBBIT*. IN THAT TIME, THE TWO ILLUSTRATORS – BOTH OF WHOM HAVE A LONG AND DISTINGUISHED CAREER AS INTERPRETERS OF TOLKIEN'S WORLDS – HAVE SHARED A STUDIO, ORIGINALLY WITHIN THE FILM'S ART DEPARTMENT, AND MORE RECENTLY AS PART OF THE WETA DIGITAL TEAM.

Production Designer Dan Hennah recalls: 'With their vast knowledge of the source material and their complementary styles, they came together really strongly at the beginning of *The Lord of the Rings* and have gone on to collaborate on *The Hobbit*. They are now such an integral part of the design team that you don't think of one without the other – it's always "John and Alan".'

As they approach the end of their work on the two trilogies they reflect on what it's been like to be closeted away together in almost monastic seclusion for so many years…

JOHN: Well, we've still got the marks of the ankle chains.

ALAN: And, of course, we beat each other with barbed chains every second Tuesday – it's a little ritual we go through.

JOHN: Absolutely – that is very creepy! But, joking apart, it is actually very stimulating, because working with somebody who's diligently drawing away on similar themes – and drawing away *very well* – means that you've got to keep concentrated and keep at it. And, perhaps not surprisingly after spending so much time together, a certain amount of osmosis goes on.

Initially, when we start designing, our approaches are quite wide ranging so that we can offer Peter as many possibilities as possible. Eventually, however, the design elements refine themselves down and the farther we get into a design, the closer and closer our views become.

ALAN: I think we each bring something a little bit different to the process. John is probably stronger on the darker, more fantastic stuff, while I'm probably a bit stronger on the more realistic side. I'm always worried about whether or not something can be easily built, but John doesn't have quite those same concerns: while I'm kind of humming and hawing, he'll take off on these great leaps of the imagination. So, the combination actually works quite well in the end: John encouraging me to be a bit bolder while, at the same time, I'm trying to give it a little bit more gravity.

RIGHT: *Production Designer Dan Hennah presents Alan & John's latest concept art to Peter for his review, with the artists standing by to explain them to the director.*

ABOVE: *John & Alan in costume as one half of the Master's band, together with John's wife, Fataneh, and a Lake-town extra carrying a pig.* ABOVE RIGHT: *Evangeline Lilly poses with John & Alan on location in the South Island.* RIGHT: *The 3D picture created by Alan & John and shown in one of the video blogs (best viewed with 3D glasses!).* BELOW: *John Howe's bowl of pencil stubs unmussed from thousands of drawings created during the project.*

JOHN: We've produced a lot of drawings for this project so far – at least 6,000 if not more. That's many miles of pencil line.

ALAN: Yes, countless pencils have perished!

JOHN: And I've actually kept all my pencil stubs! It's like –

ALAN: – which is a typically John-thing to do.

JOHN: Is it really? Well, there must be a good 250 of them, easily.

ALAN: How many, *exactly*?

JOHN: Well, I haven't counted recently, but I've already filled one jar with them and started on another. I'll count them one day and we can auction them for charity. Or I'll get someone at Weta Workshop to glue them all together and make a sculpture!

ALAN: I think a kind of bed of nails would be more appropriate! As you might guess, we have tended to get a bit isolated working on this project and not always notice what's going on in the rest of the world. Terrible events are going on out there, but what's the worst that can happen to a couple of artists having fun –

JOHN: Unless it's having a little existential problem with their art –

ALAN: – or getting a bit uptight because a roof beam on one of the sets doesn't look quite the way it does in a drawing? It's all pretty small beer in the grand scheme of things.

JOHN: Yes, it could be worse! I mean it is quite extraordinary to have a job where you simply spend all your time drawing subjects that you absolutely adore.

ALAN: I don't think we've had any bad moments at all –

JOHN: The hardest thing, perhaps, is letting go of an idea, when it's simply not working. Usually it will come out as something different – and often better. But we do sometimes look at the calendar and think how long ago it was that we did anything that was not for a movie. When we finally get out, we will be like prisoners emerging from jail after six years' hard labour! Getting back to normal life is going to be difficult.

ALAN: You mean, a 'normal life' of painting fantasy pictures!

SHARED VISION

Christopher Lee
SARUMAN OF THE BUSY EYEBROWS

'IT IS EXTRAORDINARY,' SAYS SIR CHRISTOPHER LEE. 'IT IS LIKE BEING IN A TIME MACHINE. BUT INSTEAD OF GOING FORWARDS WE'RE GOING BACKWARDS IN TIME!'

Christopher is in London, back in the flowing, snow-white robes, bearded and be-wigged and ready to film shots of Saruman, head of the order of Wizards, for scenes to be later staged in New Zealand with the other members of the White Council, Galadriel, Gandalf and Elrond.

'It's an amazing experience,' says the veteran actor who, among many other distinctions, is listed in *The Guinness Book of World Records* as the most prolific screen actor. His appearance in *The Battle of the Five Armies* will be his 276th performance.

A long-time aficionado of the writings of J.R.R. Tolkien, Christopher still regularly re-reads the books and well remembers encountering his literary hero in the author's favourite haunt, *The Eagle and Child* pub in Oxford. A return to Tolkien's realm, therefore, finds Christopher is in his element: 'It never entered my head for a second that I would be in *The Hobbit*, because Saruman is not in the book, but fortunately for me – and hopefully the audience agrees – they decided to bring Saruman back. The huge difference is in the nature of his personality and behaviour. This time it's a totally different presentation of the character: he is the original Saruman, the noble, decent, helpful master of the Wizards fighting on the side of good.'

The actor is, perhaps, being a little disingenuous in this description, since we learn from Tolkien's wider writings that when the White Council was established at the request of the Lady Galadriel, she was opposed to its being under

BELOW: *Sir Christopher Lee (and his eyebrows) in action as Saruman.* **OPPOSITE:** *The White Wizard looks tickled pink to receive a surprise gift of his seat-name, which has been inscribed to him from Peter & Fran.*

THE OFFICIAL MOVIE GUIDE

Gandalf – rather as a headmaster might admonish a senior pupil, perhaps with an occasional indulgent smile: "Can't you understand?", "Why did you do this?", "I don't approve…" and so on. But with no sense of evil or Saruman's later desire for Middle-earth domination.'

An actor who has worked with more directors than most of his profession, Christopher enjoyed being reunited with Peter Jackson. 'He is great because he never lets anything through unless it's exactly what he wants. He's definitive on that, which is extremely important.'

There was, however, the question of those eyebrows so deftly reconfigured into a frown of displeasure or arched in disbelief. 'Apparently, it's a habit of mine. I'm not really aware of this but I'm a bit of an eyebrow performer, in Peter's opinion. Maybe it's something that comes naturally to me: I ask, "What did you say?" and there's the questioning eyebrow. Anyway, Peter kept on saying, "You're doing your eyebrow-acting again!" So I had to cut that right down.'

There is a beat and Christopher adds: 'It was, of course, all a joke!' And up go the eyebrows. 'You see?' he laughs. 'There I go again – eyebrows!'

the leadership of Saruman and that Gandalf began to have his suspicions of the White Wizard's true intentions long before Saruman's treachery was unmasked.

Perhaps those suspicions are as yet unfounded, or possibly Saruman is merely biding his time; for Christopher Lee the character's motives are unambiguous: 'As Peter put it to me, Saruman talks to the others – and especially

⁌ Apparently, it's a habit of mine. I'm not really aware of but I'm a bit of an eyebrow performer, in Peter's opinion. Maybe it's something that comes naturally to me ⁋

THE STORIES OF SARUMAN

'Christopher Lee cares deeply about these books,' says Peter Jackson of the actor reprising his role as Saruman the White, 'and, more than that, is something of a Tolkien scholar, so it was great that he was able to come back to the role and play him at a time before Saruman fell into darkness.'

Sir Christopher's scenes were filmed at Pinewood Studios in London, and reuniting actor and director provided Peter with many opportunities to enjoy the actor's renowned talent as a raconteur. Laughing at the memory, Peter says: 'I love Christopher's stories and I don't think I've ever heard the same one twice. But Caro Cunningham, our First Assistant Director and Producer, has rather come to dread the moment when Christopher and I get together on set, because it's her job to keep everything moving along – shoot a shot, set up, shoot the next one and so on – that's her job and she's very, very good at doing it. The trouble is, Christopher's stories are somewhat *Lord of the Rings*-like in their epic scope and length.'

Shooting in hired studios in London meant that any delays would be costly, so the pressure was on to curtail overlong spells of conversation between director and star. 'I tend to be happy to sit there with the crew standing around, listening to Christopher's stories, and they are always fascinating because of the extraordinary experiences he has had in his long life and his recollections of the many people he's met, but this can take up valuable filming time. In London – having learned, I guess, from past experience – Caro cleverly built some story time into the schedule!'

FAMILY SNAPSHOT

Peter Jackson has a lot of cameras and he knows them all by name: 'We've got forty-eight cameras in total which, of course, means twenty-four 3D rigs. With that many cameras, it's useful to be able to identify them all so we keep track of which camera is where or in case we need to swap one out or have it repaired. Rather than use numbers we've given them all names and they are all quite personal… One's called Bill, named after my Dad; then there's Walter and Arthur, the names of my grandfathers. Ronald is my uncle, Stuart, Frank, Henry and Sidney are other uncles and Emily was Fran's grandmother. Perkins and Richie-Poo were Fran's dogs when she was young and Tricky-Roo was a 'Peke' who belonged to her aunt and uncle. Timmy was my pet tabby cat that I had as a kid and Fergus is the name of one of our pugs. There are also four cameras called John, Paul, George and Ringo who are *not* relations of mine… I honestly don't know why we *need* twenty-four cameras – after all, you can only use one at a time. Never mind, I suppose, if we wanted to, we could always shoot twenty-four different movies at the same time!'

CLOCKWISE FROM TOP LEFT: *Cameras in action: filming the refugees' makeshift shelters; skimming over the heads of Elven soldiers; Director of Photography Andrew Lesnie shoots a dusty crowd scene; a close audience with King Thorin; Jimmy Nesbitt entertains Dean O'Gorman, John Callen, Aidan Turner & Peter Jackson; Andy Serkis checks his monitor; Fili rides towards the camera; (left to right) 3D Camera Supervisor Gareth Daley, Editor Jabez Olssen & Andrew Lesnie are amused to learn they're now filming 'Red Dragon'; and Richard Armitage and 'George' the camera take a good look at one another.*

ABOVE: *Though a hitherto unseen location in Middle-earth, the Woodland Realm, being home to Legolas (inset), offered an opportunity to provide subtle links back to the music of* **The Lord of the Rings** *trilogy.* **OPPOSITE:** *Similarly, grand statements, such as the Dwarves' arrival at Erebor, provided opportunities to recall moments in the previous score.*

Explaining how he achieved this contrast, Howard says: 'In Rivendell, the most majestic and learned of these Elf worlds, the music is mainly symphonic and choral. I used a lot of singing in the Elvish language of Quenya and the voices were a continuous part of the atmosphere of the place. In Lothlórien, I used fewer voices and the music, while still orchestral, had the addition of Eastern folk instruments such as the sarangi, a bowed lute, that helped introduce a more exotic sound. With the Mirkwood kingdom, whilst wanting to preserve the mystery of the Elves, I decided to use a choral sound only very lightly. The resulting score is less quiet and, maybe, not as beautiful as those

other compositions, but that is an indication that the place is more ambiguous and potentially perilous.'

Whilst the Woodland Realm represented a hitherto unvisited Middle-earth location, it had, as Howard points out, the benefit of being the home of a character with whom *Rings* fans were already well acquainted: 'The environment may be unfamiliar but we are meeting an important character there who we are going to meet again later in *Rings*. So it was necessary to connect the Legolas we encounter in Mirkwood with the member of the Fellowship of the Ring who we already know to be someone who is brave and true.'

For Howard, the character of Tauriel allowed him to give a more favourable dimension to an essentially hostile world: 'Tauriel has a piece of music that is keyed to her relationship with Kili and another that depicts her as the Elf-warrior and action heroine. Chiefly used in the fight and battle scenes; it is also developed for her more tender moments and even in her interaction with King Thranduil.'

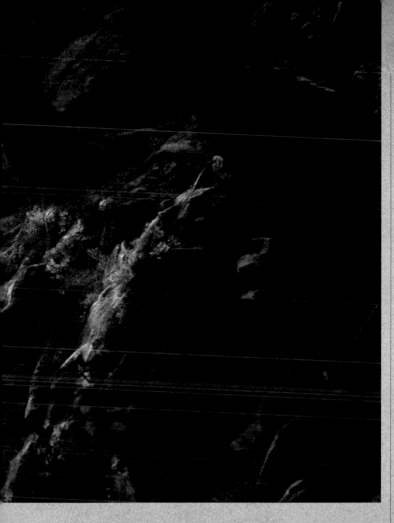

ever-extending exploration through the use of instruments from the four compass points of our own world.'

The Lord of the Rings yielded those opportunities as the Fellowship journeyed south, passing through the lands of Rohan and Gondor. *The Hobbit* provides another community, this time to the north, with Lake-town. 'Although a region populated by men, it is,' says Howard 'unlike those inhabited by the horse-masters of Edoras or the people living in the grandeur of Minas Tirith, lacking the nobility of either of those places.'

Lake-town is a polyglot society of fishermen, traders and travellers, and its musical theme recalls the sea shanties that have, for generations, been the work songs of communities living on or by the water. There was an additional inspiration, as Howard explains with a laugh: 'My music originates from a thought Peter Jackson shared with me that the atmosphere of Lake-town was like a smuggling operation in eighteenth-century Cornwall! As a result, there's a decidedly underworld feel to the town and what goes on there.'

Introduced in *The Desolation of Smaug*, the character of Bard becomes more musically fully defined in *The Battle of the Five Armies* when, as Howard explains, the strength and courage of the Bowman of Lake-town is tested against the rage of Smaug the Dragon. 'Although there are thematic links to the music I wrote for Bard's ancestor, Girion the Lord of Dale, who also battled with Smaug, I initially had to keep his character enigmatic. I couldn't reveal everything about Bard at first because, when we first encounter him, we are not quite sure where he stands and it was important to maintain that sense of mystery in his music.'

The Hobbit trilogy has allowed Howard to do more than simply return to his earlier musical depiction of Middle-earth. 'What is so great about Tolkien's writing,' he says, 'and what is such a wonderful gift to a composer is being able to use instruments from all over the world to describe the cultures as Tolkien keeps expanding the story across his world. My aim has been to reflect that

just begun to understand the true significance of the Arkenstone,' says Howard. 'In *An Unexpected Journey* and *The Desolation of Smaug*, the Arkenstone theme was little more than a few fragments – fleeting glimmers and flashes of light – but it is an object that is still to reveal its true identity and significance, something that will be musically fulfilled in *The Battle of the Five Armies*.'

The concluding part of *The Hobbit* sees the full power of both Smaug the Magnificent and the shadowy figure of the Necromancer who has now been revealed as the former incarnation of the Dark Lord, Sauron.

For the Dwarvish kingdom of Erebor, Howard Shore's inspiration began with a return to some of his earlier compositions: 'In *The Lord of the Rings*, we had scenes in Moria and at Balin's Tomb: I went back to those pieces and wrote off them to make sure that I left the musical equivalent of a trail of breadcrumbs to show that what I was writing for Erebor could connect to those themes from the earlier trilogy.'

At the heart of Thorin's realm lies its greatest prize, a gem of unbelievable beauty and worth. 'We have only

In creating a musical theme for the elemental force of nature that is the Dragon and the cascades of shifting gold that fills his lair, the score makes use of a diverse and complex choice of instrumentation, many of which reflecting the vibrant music associated with Eastern instrumentation: 'In addition to the full symphony orchestra, I used the sarangi and the dilruba – a sitar played with a bow – together with Chinese percussion, Japanese drumming on the taiko, Japanese hanging cymbals (an instrument I had used in

OPPOSITE: *Dark moments call for dark music, such as the Orcs departing Dol Guldur* (top). *Similarly, scenes featuring dark characters such as Bolg will contain fragments of music linking them to Mordor and to Sauron* (bottom). ABOVE: *When scoring the Erebor scenes Composer Howard Shore created a musical 'trail of breadcrumbs' back to the Moria scenes in* The Fellowship of the Ring.

Rings for 'The Paths of the Dead') and a new component in the *Hobbit* score, the Indonesian gamelan with its unique combination of highly individual percussive instruments.'

Like a number of musical themes, that for the Necromancer has been gradually taking form across the trilogy, as Howard explains: 'Though not yet fully formed, the Necromancer has fragments from my themes for Mordor and Sauron in *The Lord of the Rings* – I drop in little hints here and there, some more bolder than others, through which you are connecting to a darkness in Middle-earth: a growing power that involves not just this mysterious entity, the Necromancer, but other dark forces too such as Azog, Bolg and the Nazgûl – the Nine Ringwraiths – for whom Peter wanted me to create something new and which are represented by a solo vocal sound.'

Unquestionably the biggest task facing Howard Shore in completing his compositions for *The Hobbit* will be scoring the climactic Battle of the Five Armies. 'One of the starting points in my preparations for the Battle of the Five Armies will be the Battle of Azanulbizar, outside Moria, featured in *An Unexpected Journey*, in which

Thorin's grandfather, Thrór was brutally slain by the Orcs. The Moria battle was strategic and so much happened in that confrontation that affected the fate and lineage of the Dwarvish race that it is a likely starting place for composition that will score the final conflict.'

When the concluding notes have been entered onto the last stave of *The Hobbit* score, Howard Shore will have composed a staggering total of some twenty hours of music chronicling Tolkien's history of Bilbo and Frodo Baggins and the War of the Ring. It will be a monumental achievement. Contemplating the end of his labours, Howard says: 'Since Peter and I talked about *The Hobbit* when we were making *The Two Towers*, it was always in our thoughts to be able to fashion the complete work, so to have eventually achieved it will be very fulfilling. Approaching the conclusion of *The Hobbit* carries me back full circle to the beginning of *The Lord of the Rings* and to the original books, because it is Tolkien who has given us his writings and allowed us to interpret them in another art form and, in my sphere, in music. That is something about which I am very happy.'

MAESTRO OF MIDDLE-EARTH

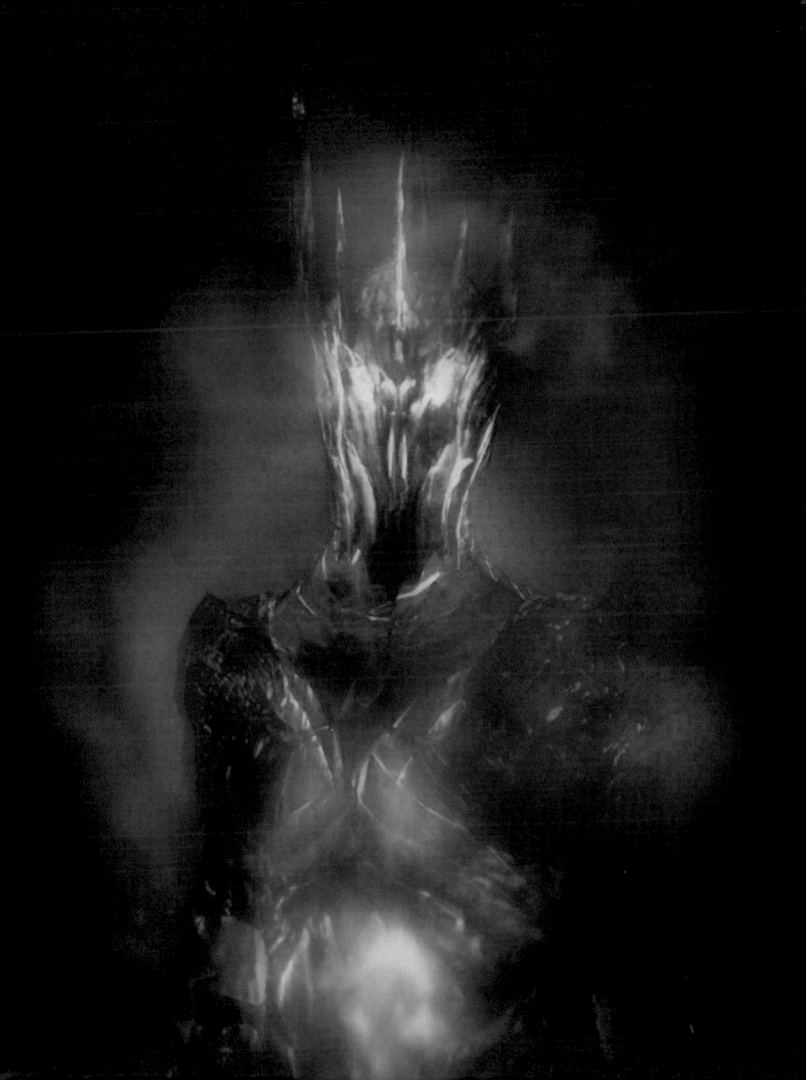

Benedict Cumberbatch
THE NECROMANCER

'IT FELT LIKE I WAS A WET PAPER TOWEL THAT WAS BEING THROWN AT THE WALL TO SEE IF ANYTHING STUCK.' BENEDICT CUMBERBATCH IS DESCRIBING HOW HE GOT THE JOB OF PROVIDING A VOICE FOR THE NECROMANCER, THE ENIGMATIC FORCE FOR EVIL THAT IS SUCH A SOURCE OF CONCERN TO THE WHITE COUNCIL IN *THE HOBBIT*.

Having auditioned, off-camera, to play the voice of Smaug – at the suggestion of Casting Director, Dan Hubbard – Benedict found himself meeting Peter Jackson, Fran Walsh and Philippa Boyens and being asked why they hadn't been able to see him on the audition tape. 'So I explained that Dan had suggested it would better if I wasn't seen, presumably in case I ruined my chances of getting the part if they'd seen my face.'

The actor was doubly confused since he had now been asked to prepare to read for four other parts, and so assumed that he had failed to get the role of Smaug. It was at this point that he expressed his feelings using the wet-paper-towel analogy. 'I told them, "I don't quite know what to focus on because there's only one part I really want to play and that's Smaug!"'

To Benedict's astonishment he was told that everyone was very happy with his Dragon-voice, but they were wondering whether he might be willing to try out in front

OPPOSITE: *The Necromancer of Dol Guldur is revealed as Sauron, the Dark Lord.* ABOVE: *Benedict Cumberbatch & Luke Evans visit Martin Freeman on set in Erebor.*

It is a very unsettling concept, as if he were non-corporeal – something intangible, somewhere between heaven and earth. But he has a force about him, a negative polarity that is almost like a black hole, drawing things and people towards him

of the camera for an additional role. One of those audition pieces was for the Necromancer and securing this second part has caused Benedict to speculate on whether he has a natural affinity with playing 'baddies'. About one thing, however, he is in no doubt: 'Villains are great, *great* characters!'

Certainly the Necromancer is intriguing and, although only briefly mentioned in Tolkien's original book, he is a major character in the history of Middle-earth; indeed his story goes back to its earliest days and reaches beyond *The Hobbit* to that of the great War of the Ring in which Bilbo's heir, Frodo, plays such a crucial role.

Giving his perspective on the Necromancer, Benedict says: 'He is an incredibly destructive, selfish and brutally motivated force of evil. He takes no prisoners and tolerates no obstruction to his plans and, in achieving them, brings about an awful lot of destruction, death, misery and nastiness.'

When dark and sinister rumours arise about the existence of a sorcerer who can summon the dead, Gandalf becomes suspicious, telling the White Council: 'There is something at work beyond the evil of Smaug, something far more powerful. We can remain blind to it but it will not be ignoring us, that I can promise you.'

Saruman dismisses the stories as absurd, saying, 'This Necromancer is nothing more than a mortal man, a conjuror dabbling in black magic.' But Gandalf suspects that the Necromancer is, in fact, none other than Sauron, past-possessor of the One Ring, long thought to have been overthrown. That, indeed, proves to be the truth, for the Dark Lord is restoring himself to his former strength and preparing to re-establish his former power.

'It is a very unsettling concept,' says Benedict, 'as if he were non-corporeal – something intangible, somewhere between heaven and earth. But he has a force about him, a negative polarity that is almost like a black hole, drawing things and people towards him. It's quite a screwy mindgame to play with – and I ended up getting very lost in it – and in terms of filming the motion-capture for the character, it was difficult to portray something illusory.'

Benedict was aided in this task by Movement Coach, Terry Notary: 'I think all voiceover actors could improve their performance by acting out the movements of their characters. Benedict is a very talented physical actor. He was down on his hands and knees playing the Dragon and it was really exciting to work with him on finding a way to visualize the Necromancer, who is the true spirit of evil and the darkest force in the films.'

In collaboration, Benedict and Terry worked at representing the Necromancer as a force that comes from and is made of shadows. The actor was videoed trying out various styles of movement while facing a bright spotlight that threw giant shadows onto a white screen. 'I walked to and fro within the light,' remembers Benedict, 'shape shifting, curling and twisting myself into different forms; experimenting with the idea of expanding and decompressing the body; and playing with the angles of the limbs – an elbow popping up where the head would usually be, then the actual head appearing out of my side – anything to produce something that was both human and, at the same time, amorphous.'

Terry Notary describes the session in this way: 'We'd push the spotlight in so his shadow would grow bigger and bigger and then – *boom!* – suddenly, Benedict would

LEFT: *This pile of bones, carefully fabricated by the Art Department, reveals the fate awaiting any visitor to Dol Guldur.* OPPOSITE: *Gandalf is forced to match power with the Necromancer.*

morph into this crunched-down character, a little human foetal form. So he's constantly changing shape from something tangible into something formless, like smoke that can never be grasped, because it has no substance.'

The tapes were run for Peter Jackson and all kinds of options were explored: 'We played some of the footage in reverse,' says Terry. 'I'd have him walk backwards, and then play it forwards at a different frame-rate to show how you could break up the rhythm and timing of the character's movements.'

In *The Battle of the Five Armies*, the Necromancer is confronted at Dol Guldur by Gandalf, Galadriel and Elrond and is required to fight. To help create these scenes on film, Benedict was kitted up with a motion-capture suit attached to bungee ropes that restrained his movements. 'He was tethered,' explains Terry, 'so that he was constantly being pulled back. This created the subtle, but powerful, effect of a force like a dark void that can never satisfy its own hunger, but sucks the energy out of everything around it in order to increase his own power.'

To add to this characterization, the Necromancer uses Black Speech, the language that, according to Tolkien, was devised by Sauron with the intention that all in Middle-earth would speak it. This dark scheme failed when, for the first time, Sauron was overthrown.

For a time, only the Nazgûl used Black Speech; however, after Sauron regained his strength – a process of healing that began at Dol Guldur – the language would become that of his servants in his stronghold, Barad-dûr, in Mordor. Only a few fragments of Black Speech appear in *The Lord of the Rings*, most significantly in the opening two lines of the 'Ring Verse' which (to everyone's horror) Gandalf quotes aloud at the Council of Elrond…

Ash nazg durbatulûk, ash nazg gimbatul,
Ash nazg thrakatulûk agh burzum-ishi krimpatul.
One Ring to rule them all, One Ring to find them,
One Ring to bring them all and in the darkness bind them.

Tolkien scholar and linguist, David Salo, who earlier served as language consultant on *The Lord of the Rings* trilogy, constructed the Black Speech dialogue for the screenplay. For Benedict, coming to terms with a new language was a challenge. 'I was a little overawed by it in the beginning,' he admits, 'but then I realized that if you speak it phonetically, it lifts off the page quite easily and I really enjoyed speaking it. It's gritty, guttural and visceral – and really rather ugly – but it has wonderful sounds to get your mouth around. We are spoiled, growing up in a culture of Shakespeare, where language helps you to achieve an emotional state. Tolkien really knew what he was doing here, because Black Speech is a language of struggle.'

As an experiment, a backwards-spoken version of the dialogue was recorded in an attempt, as Benedict explains, to create a vocal equivalent of the character's way of moving: 'Normal speech is made by air vibrating over your vocal chords as you breathe out; but instead of making sounds through an exhalation of breath, we wanted to give the impression that they were made by an inhalation, as if everything about the Necromancer is done inwardly, rather than projected outwards. I recorded the words backwards, trying to match the intonations I

would use if I were speaking in the normal way. First, I would record it forwards and then reverse the process, so if I had built to a crescendo, I would start with that crescendo and work backwards to something more neutral as a finishing point. Because it's unnatural, it's a very creepy sound: uncanny and unnerving – in fact, everything that the character should be.'

The actor relished the experimentation: 'There was a lot of freedom to play with, so I recorded the Black Speech forwards, backwards and at several different pitches. I also did English versions, because the Necromancer has the ability to be a projection of those in his presence. Sometimes the words were distinct and clipped and then they would recede into something almost abstract. There were wonderfully poetic moments where it's almost nothing more than breath, and then in come all those consonants again, with a kind of terrible anger. The aim was to give the Sound Department lots of options to ease in and out of these really odd textures.'

Nevertheless, the process was not an entirely pleasant one: 'It was rather horrible: like playing with voodoo or black magic! There were moments when, to clear myself of the feeling, I just had to go off and speak the Queen's English and have a cup of tea!'

And, when that beverage had worked its own unique restorative charm, Benedict would inevitably find himself reflecting on the character he is really portraying in the role of the Necromancer: 'It's the beginning of the all-seeing Eye of Sauron. That's an amazing thing! Watching *The Lord of the Rings* trilogy again now, I think: "It's really all about this evil dude who I'm playing in *The Hobbit*. So, actually, it's all about me!'

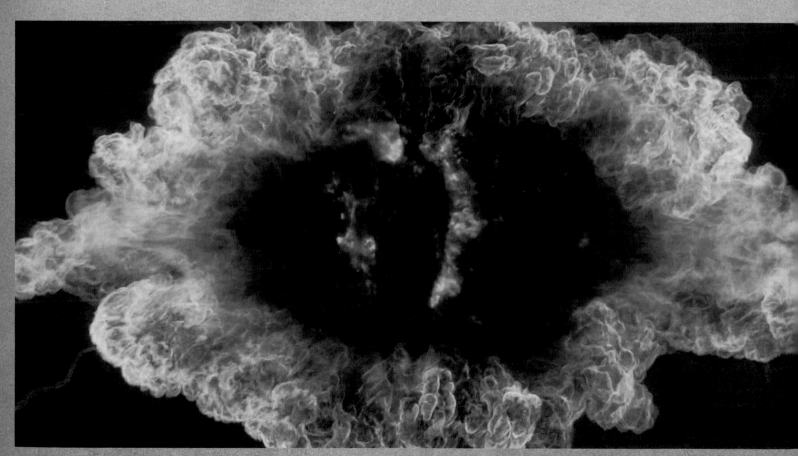

THE RISE OF
THE NECROMANCER

In *An Unexpected Journey*, Saruman responded with scepticism to Gandalf's suggestion that Sauron had returned: 'The enemy is defeated,' he assured the White Council. 'Sauron is vanquished. He can never regain his full strength.'

Gandalf, however, is certain that the destructive force, referred to as The Necromancer, which is abroad in Middle-earth signifies nothing less than the return of an old enemy dating back to a time before time.

Sauron was one of the immortal spirits who were created by the Supreme Being, Eru Ilúvatar, and aided in the fashioning of the universe. Of these spirits, the most powerful were the Valar and those with lesser powers, the Maiar.

J.R.R. Tolkien tells us that one of the Valar, named Melkor, rebelled against Eru Ilúvatar and became the source of all evil in Middle-earth. Renamed Morgoth by the Elves, this fallen spirit was served by many beings that he corrupted or created, among them Balrogs, Dragons, Werewolves, Vampires and monstrous Spiders. His chief lieutenant was one of the Maiar, and another rebellious spirit – Sauron.

After many struggles, Morgoth was overthrown and cast out beyond the world, but Sauron escaped and hid and began to rebuild his powers, forging the One Ring in an attempt to ensnare and rule the Elves, Dwarves and Men who wore the Rings of Power. An alliance between Elves and Men defeated Sauron, the One Ring was taken from him and, for a time, he was vanquished, his spirit fleeing his body and going into hiding.

Years passed and the One Ring was lost – only to be later claimed by a hobbit-like creature called Sméagol. Meanwhile, a corrupting shadow was lengthening across the land and Gandalf, aware that a malevolent influence had established a stronghold on what came to be called Dol Guldur – the 'hill of sorcery' – correctly deduced that the so-called Necromancer was none other than Sauron…

WIZARD FACTS

Although the peoples of Middle-earth were initially unaware of the fact, the Wizards – or *Istari* as they are known in the Elvish language of Quenya – had been sent from the Valar, the Lords of the West, to assist in the struggle against the rise of Sauron.

The Istari were five in number, and were known by the colour of their robes. Saruman the White was considered to be head of the order and was followed by the two Blue Wizards, Radagast the Brown and the last-comer, Gandalf the Grey.

Late on the scene he may have been, but Gandalf became a prime mover in the affairs of Middle-earth, culminating in the War of the Ring. Saruman, too, played his part, though it was to be in the role of deceiver and traitor, while Radagast, who is only briefly mentioned in Tolkien's *The Hobbit* and *The Lord of the Rings*, was distracted from his mission by his love of bird and beast; although, as recorded in *The Fellowship of the Ring*, by sending the great Eagle to Saruman's stronghold, Orthanc, with news for Gandalf, he unwittingly aided the Grey Wizard's escape.

Of the other two Wizards little is recorded other than that they travelled into the Eastern lands of Middle-earth and never returned. In one of Tolkien's additional narratives, he speculates on whether they might have perished or been ensnared by the wiles of Sauron. 'They had no names,' says the author, 'save *Ithryn Luin* "The Blue Wizards".' But elsewhere in his writings he does give them names: in one source as Alatar and Pallando and, in another, Morinehtar and Rómestámo.

This uncertainty explains a remark made by Gandalf in *The Hobbit: An Unexpected Journey* when answering Bilbo's question about the wizards of Middle-earth. 'The greatest of our order,' he says, 'is Saruman the White. And then there are the two Blue Wizards…' at which point Gandalf breaks off, looks thoughtful and adds: 'Do you know, I've quite forgotten their names.'

DOL GULDUR

ALAN LEE RECALLS WORKING ON THE DESIGN FOR DOL GULDUR THAT UNDERWENT A SIGNIFICANT DEVELOPMENT DURING THE COURSE OF THE TRILOGY: 'THE BRIEF GLIMPSES SEEN IN *AN UNEXPECTED JOURNEY* DIDN'T PERMIT THE OPPORTUNITY TO ESTABLISH THE SCALE AND COMPLEXITY OF THE BUILDING THAT WOULD BE REQUIRED FOR A THOROUGH EXPLORATION IN LATER SCENES. DOL GULDUR HAD A PHYSICAL SET FOR SPECIFIC ACTION SHOTS BUT THE IMMENSITY OF THE BUILDING WAS CREATED AS A DIGITAL EXTENSION.

'My previous experience of working on intricate structures had involved the use of maquettes and miniatures, all based on drawings, and then created by a team of model-makers. Working on a CG environment is very different because it allows for added flexibility for the animators and others in the post-production process. However, because my imagination is still too analogue, I found it easier to draw up a modular plan for the structure, so that it could be extensive, without involving an overly daunting amount of digital modelling work. Essentially, Dol Guldur comprises two basic tower designs and a section of wall that could be replicated, with variations, to create the impression of a vast environment. For myself, I justify the changes between Dol Guldur in the first and later movies on the basis of Gandalf's description: "It's a place of illusion"!'

John Howe comments: 'I've come to realize that every time Gandalf meets a bad guy he does so on a bridge! Why can't they just have a punch-up on a flat floor for a change?'

Paul Randall, Scale Double
TALL ORDERS

'THANKS TO TOLKIEN, WHO CREATED ALL THOSE WIZARDS, DWARVES, HOBBITS AND HUMANS, I HAVE A JOB!' SO SAYS PAUL RANDALL, WHOSE JOB IS MAKING MARTIN FREEMAN, RICHARD ARMITAGE AND OTHERS LOOK SMALL – OR, AT LEAST, A LOT SMALLER THAN THEY TRULY ARE.

Measuring up at seven-feet tall or, as he says, 'seven-foot-*one* on a good day,' there was a time when Paul Randall was best known for being New Zealand's tallest policeman. Then in 1999, Peter Jackson embarked on filming *The Lord of the Rings* and Paul found himself presented with a new and unexpected career opportunity.

In order to create the illusion that the actors playing Bilbo, Frodo, Sam and Gimli were, like their characters, of restricted growth it was necessary for scenes where Gandalf and Boromir had to interact with hobbits and Dwarves to have someone considerably taller than Ian McKellen or Sean Bean. So Paul would don an outsized version of their

costumes and stand in for the actors. Between times, he served as a Third Assistant Director: 'I'd have my radio and all my gear and be doing my job,' he recalls, 'and I'd suddenly get the call: "Paul, come and be Gandalf!" – or it might be Boromir or someone else – and I'd have to run, get changed and jump into the scene without really having any idea what I was doing!'

That was Paul Randall's entrée to the movie business and when production began on *The Hobbit* he took unpaid leave from the police force and returned to Middle-earth where 'Tall Paul', as he is known, has once again been providing large-scale substitution for Gandalf, Bard and even, fleetingly, Thranduil.

'What Peter Jackson would *really* like,' says Paul, 'is for me to be over *eight*-feet tall, but we have ways to get around the fact that I'm not really quite tall enough: sometimes I might be on a platform to get the correct scale, at other times it's down to where the camera is placed.'

Paul's chief role remains Gandalf the Grey and, having worked with Ian McKellen, on and off, for almost fifteen years now, he has learned how to replicate the actor's Wizard persona, despite being thirty years his junior: 'Ian is such a fantastic actor who uses small, often subtle, gestures and hand movements and I try to replicate those as accurately as possible. He's a little bent over, leaning on his staff, and his walk is a little bit rickety; he's always got his sword and holds it in a very particular fashion, and when he is at ease he will often stand with his thumb in his belt. I don't often get much time for preparation, but luckily, after all these years, I have got to know his character so well that I just do it!'

Just as important as mastering Ian's physical portrayal of Gandalf is the ability to convey a sense of the character's

OPPOSITE: *With Peter's camera directed at Martin Freeman's face, Paul is out of shot from the shoulders up.* RIGHT: *Even at seven feet tall, Paul must stand on a platform to correctly tower over Richard Armitage.* BELOW: *Paul Randall, out of costume but wearing the uniform of his day job.*

thoughts and emotions. 'I need to understand what he is thinking and feeling,' says Paul. 'Is he anxious? Does he know what he's doing? Is he trying to keep something from somebody? Those are the things that I am most interested in getting right. And there are other considerations, one of which is that I have to be very aware of where the cameras are at any time, because they don't want to see my face as it makes things more difficult later on. So I have to try to look like Gandalf and act natural while keeping my face out of shot, all of which takes a bit of practice.'

An average day as a tall Gandalf double begins with costume and make-up: 'Everything is up-scaled: big hat, cloak and boots and a massive staff. I've also got a huge wig and a beard that's a horrible monstrous thing. I don't really enjoy the hairiness of Gandalf – it's hot and itchy – but it looks good and I really like the character itself because it's the one I'm most familiar with. I've been on set when Peter has said, "It's uncanny how Paul moves like Ian," and Ian has said, "Yes, I really don't need to be here anymore!" Which I take as a real compliment.'

Providing Luke Evans with a tall double is a rather different challenge: 'Bard is a young fella, very strong and confident who, unlike Gandalf, stands straight and walks with big, long, purposeful strides. It's been interesting to study his character and Luke's performance and to get to wear a different costume.'

In terms of wardrobe, Paul's most interesting experience of scale-doubling was standing in for Lee Pace as Thranduil. 'I was wearing a flowing silver robe,' he laughs, 'big silver boots, beautiful long blond hair and a completely whited-out face. Apparently, however, this wasn't – for me – a good look: I walked onto the set and everyone burst out laughing. It was quite embarrassing but luckily you'll never get to see that!'

It is a curious job pretending to be other people being other people, which is why Paul enjoys the occasional opportunity to be an extra in the films: 'You might say,

"Oh, just an extra," but it's good for me because I actually get my face on camera, which is nice, and I quite enjoy giving a performance of my own rather than trying to duplicate someone else's.'

With filming coming to an end, Paul is getting ready to head back to join his colleagues in the police; he admits to always watching the finished films with an eye to spotting his appearances: 'I'm usually watching out for myself, and my family and friends are always trying to pinpoint where I am! But hopefully I'm good enough that no one out there will be able to know when it's Ian and when it's me. If that's the case, then I've done my job well.'

THE UPS & DOWNS OF DALE

'TRY IMAGINING A TIBETAN CITY IN THE SWISS ALPS – ON THE ITALIAN SIDE.' CONCEPT ARTIST, JOHN HOWE, IS TALKING ABOUT THE CREATION OF THE CITY OF DALE, WHICH IS SEEN IN THE TRILOGY IN TWO WILDLY DIFFERENT INCARNATIONS.

Characters in J.R.R. Tolkien's *The Hobbit* repeatedly speak of the splendours of the Northern city of men that once proudly stood within the shadow of the Lonely Mountain, and of the terrible devastation that fell upon it with the coming of the Dragon, Smaug.

'Welcome to the city of Dale,' says Production Designer, Dan Hennah, standing in the midst of the huge set on Mount Crawford, outside Wellington. 'It is probably our biggest set on *The Hobbit* and it's certainly been the most fun to build. Ten weeks ago this was just a bare parking lot; now we have a busy city here as it would have looked on a mid-summer market day, with heaps of people having a good time in the sunshine.'

Indeed, within the next twenty-four hours, the streets and squares will be thronging with extras representing the happy folk of Dale: toy-sellers, market stall-holders, folk happily going about their daily lives untroubled, and laughing children riding a carousel and flying kites – including one in the ominously portentous form of a dragon.

'Dale as it is seen in the prologue to *An Unexpected Journey* is a very fertile environment,' explains Dan, 'and so water is a prominent feature, with fountains, waterfalls and troughs with running water in the streets. It is an orchard city and one of the many things that has got to be right before we start filming is the foliage.'

That task is the responsibility of the Greens Department. On every movie shoot – and especially on films like *The Hobbit* and *The Lord of the Rings* – 'Greens' are responsible to the Production Designer and the Art Department for set-dressing, involving all kinds and combinations of trees, shrubs, plants, flowers, grass and, obviously, greenery. This might require relocating real trees into studio settings, or erecting artificial trees on location such as the famous Hobbiton 'Party Tree' featured in both trilogies. Quite often the greensman's skill lies in cleverly combining the real with the artificial.

'This is probably the most enjoyable part of our job,' says Greensmaster Simon Lowe, 'as we add the final finishing touches and the whole set comes to life.' Those touches include planting flowers and adding fruit to the trees in the orchard and vines in the vineyard.

The trees are a mix of those created by sculptors and those made by nature. 'We are trying to blur the line between the real and the artificial,' says Simon, 'so we will be putting real fruit on the artificial trees and artificial fruit on the real trees!'

The numbers, as always on these films, are staggering: 'We've made 16,000 sprays of artificial foliage and

OPPOSITE: *Gus Hunter's sumptuous concept painting reveals Dale in all its glory.* ABOVE: *Two of the many concept drawings of Dale made by Alan Lee* (top) *and John Howe* (middle) *exploring a diverse range of architectural styles.* LEFT: *Production Designer Dan Hennah reviews a detailed model of part of the city with Art Director Simon Bright* (left) *and Set Decorator Ra Vincent* (right).

LEFT: *Ra Vincent's colouring of a concept drawing* (top) *provides the Greens Department with visual cues on how to dress the set* (bottom).

14,000 mulberries; then there are 3,500 apples, 2,000 pears, 500 lemons, 200 persimmons and a fair few tangerines, some made and some bought. At this time of year in New Zealand there is actually a lot of fruit available and when you are talking in terms of the volume we are after, it's a lot cheaper for us to use the real thing rather than make artificial versions.'

The concept for Dale was only reached after John Howe and Alan Lee had made a great many exploratory drawings, taking their inspiration from architectural styles referencing a diverse range of cultures.

'We came up with a look for Dale,' says Alan, 'that feels a bit more Eastern and, because it is close to the Mountain, we considered the architecture of various mountainous regions.' The result is a conglomeration of tall, tapering, buildings with shallow, pitched, red-tiled roofs, interspersed with towers and domes.

He continues: 'Dale is essentially built from stone with

wooden windows and cantilevered wooden balconies; we wanted to have lots of wood so that there was plenty of stuff for Smaug to set alight!'

Whilst Dale was never intended for any actual geographical location to be identifiable, John reveals that people seeing the set instantly made their own comparisons between Dale and places in our world: 'Everyone said it reminded them of somewhere – Nepal, Northern Italy, Croatia, Latvia – but every individual had a different destination in mind.'

It doesn't much matter where it reminds you of because it isn't going to look like it for long. A dramatic change is on the way: Dale is shortly to be scheduled for demolition – by dragon. Dan Hennah explains: 'As soon as we have shot the scenes for the prologue to *An Unexpected Journey* we will be turning this beautiful city into a post-apocalyptic – or, at least, post-*Smaug* – ruin with everything looking old, charred and devastated.'

Fast-forward 170 years by Middle-earth reckoning (but just three weeks in movie-making time) and Set Decorator, Ra Vincent, is checking out the changes that Dale has undergone which will be witnessed by Bilbo, Thorin and Company as they pass through the wrecked city.

'This was an interesting challenge,' says Ra, 'to go back and ruin what has been so painstakingly created on set. Teams have been in to break things up, knock holes in the masonry and give everything a burnt look and now Greens have returned and are starting to plant a mass of tangled trees.'

'This was a really nice old orchard,' says Brian Massey, the Greens Art Director, 'but now it is totally beaten up. The gates have been smashed open and burnt as Smaug roared over them with his destructive fireballs. Everything is tainted and dying. The trees are the few remnants that have tried to keep growing but have largely been unsuccessful.'

Brian and his crew aim to create a look that is in striking contrast to the bountiful place previously seen: 'Basically, we are trashing a lot of the trees – being winter time they have lost their leaves – and we are also putting in extra growth of the kind that would have grown up around buildings that haven't been attended to for so many years. We have planted weeds and briars and have made big ropey artificial vines – great tortuous creepers that we will have growing up through steps and balconies and into windows and doorways. We are trying to create

RIGHT: *Art Director Simon Bright visits the Dale set, now ruined to show the desolation of Smaug (top); fake cobwebs and ageing by the set dressers ensure that this interior looks really derelict (middle); the huge exterior set is dressed with newly planted weeds, tangled trees and fake snow to reflect that winter has come (bottom).*

as much interaction as we can between the trees and the vines and the architecture.'

Brian now leads the way to a part of Dale only glimpsed in the prologue – the Great Hall. Strongly built, the city's civic centre has suffered only minimal damage apart from the all-too-visible scars left by Smaug's fire; but soon to be added are indications of the unrelenting ravages of time: 'There will be trees growing in the interior and coming out and climbing up the façade of the building.'

A few final embellishments have still to be arranged before filming recommences: 'There's the remnants of a spring-fed fountain,' says Brian, 'and when we film here it will be leaking and the streets will be running with water and slime; there will be piles of rubble, burnt remains, a mummified body and a fall of winter snow – everything that will generally add to a feeling of a place that, whatever its glories once were, is now miserable and uninhabitable.'

Contemplating the transformation of Dale, Ra Vincent finds himself in something of a dilemma: 'It's been quite an experience, breaking down what was a gorgeous sunny day set into this really cold, slightly creepy, uninviting city, which has seen better days. But the trouble is, I'm not quite sure which I like better: the beautiful Dale or the trashed one!'

THE UPS & DOWNS OF DALE

Making Believe

ASK ASSISTANT ART DIRECTOR, MICHAEL SMALE, WHAT THE WORK OF THE ART DEPARTMENT AND THE DESIGNERS OF WETA DIGITAL HAVE GIVEN TO *THE HOBBIT* AND HE'LL ANSWER WITH A WORD – *BELIEVABILITY...*

The aim, says Michael, has been to make Middle-earth as believable as our own world: 'We want it to feel like a real place, to immerse the viewer in the realm of the story. As well as creating unique architectural and decorative styles for the peoples of Middle-earth, we also try to consider how they would live their day-to-day lives, and give them histories, which helps to add detail and credibility to the environments in which they exist. We consider how long they've lived there and what the effects of age and wear would have had on their surroundings. We make sure that any surfaces at street level are more worn than those higher up, that the paint on buildings is more faded on the sunny side and that stair treads are more worn in the middle than the extremities.'

Another consideration is where a culture's food comes from: 'In Dale there are terraced agricultural crops surrounding the city, in Lake-town the food is generally brought in by boat and then sold to the people at markets.

This influenced how we laid out the town plan – we had a market district located near the boat docks, as well as a warehouse district for food storage, and a district on the town outskirts where they processed the fish. In the case of Lake-town, we also considered what the inhabitants would do for a living and how this would impact on the way they lived. This led to the creation of a boat-building district with dry docks, a fishermen's district on the outskirts which was generally a poor area dressed with fishing equipment, a merchants' district with bigger, more ornate buildings, a military area where the soldiers were billeted in barracks. Within the town's market areas we assigned buildings to specific trades and professions – shops for bakers, greengrocers, premises for a blacksmith, weavers, tanners and, of course, a pub.'

So thorough was the thinking behind the planning of the towns and cities that attention was even paid to plumbing and sanitation: 'Where exactly does the inhabitants' waste go? In Dale, an aqueduct from the adjacent mountain range supplies the town with fresh water and there is a sewage and drainage system which feeds into a river below. In Goblin-town, at the opposite end of the hygiene spectrum, the Goblins were such uncouth creatures that they just defecated off their gangways onto whatever was below, so we textured the walkways to ensure they were more "poo"-covered the further down you got. In Lake-town the people emptied their waste into the lake, so we made the water suitably dirty looking with foul-looking floating objects. There were also a lot of dogs and animals in Lake-town, so we added in little piles of dog faeces in places along the walkways.'

Even when settings were being created in a computer rather than in actuality the

OPPOSITE: (Left to right) *Set Decorator Ra Vincent, Production Designer Dan Hennah & Art Director Simon Bright.*
ABOVE: *Meticulous planning and incredible attention to detail are needed to turn a studio set into a living environment.*
BELOW: *The entire contents of Bilbo's home had to be transported from the studios to Matamata to be filmed outside the Bag End exterior set (left); the director, cast & crew stand beneath Dale's aqueduct (right).*

same imperative for authenticity was applied, as Michael explains: 'For the natural environment – trees, terrain, lakes – which needed to be built digitally we always found existing reference, wherever possible, within New Zealand which could be digitally scanned and which helped give a more "real" quality. We had large areas of high resolution scanned terrain, which then got adapted to fit our purposes. For the Goblin caverns we searched for existing rocks with the pitted, eroded quality we needed. John Howe and I found some great ones in Karaka Bay, just five minutes' drive from our office, which were scanned and photographed. For the Dale Valley, where the Battle of the Five Armies takes place, we used large sections of scans of the Rock and Pillar landscape in the South Island, augmented with other rock features and rivers. It is part of the philosophy of the production that, by adding these extra layers of detail, it helps bring the sets to life, and hopefully enhance the story.'

THE ARKENSTONE

'IT'S LIKE STEALING A PEA OFF THE PLATE OF HANNIBAL LECTER!' PETER JACKSON IS TALKING ABOUT THE CHALLENGE FACING BURGLAR BILBO IN PURLOINING THE ARKENSTONE FROM SMAUG'S DRAGON HORDE.

An heirloom of priceless value to the Dwarves of the race of Durin, the Arkenstone was discovered shortly after Thráin I had established the Kingdom of Erebor beneath the Lonely Mountain. Tolkien has Thráin's descendant, Thorin Oakenshield, describe the stone as being 'worth more than a river of gold in itself'.

Appropriately described as 'The Heart of the Mountain', the Arkenstone is first glimpsed in *The Hobbit* film trilogy in the prologue to *An Unexpected Journey*. Its significance begins to be understood in *The Desolation of Smaug* and becomes of great importance to the storyline of *The Battle of the Five Armies*.

'The Arkentstone is the symbol of all things Dwarven,' says Peter, 'and whilst it doesn't have any magical powers, it represents the various Dwarf kingdoms that have been scattered around Middle-earth and which may, one day, be reunited around it.'

Clearly a lot of thought needed to go into designing and creating how the Arkenstone would appear in the films.

'It's a translucent white, polished stone,' says Props Making Supervisor, Paul Gray, 'and some people might say it's not the most interesting thing that we made, but it is a prop that is pivotal to the story and had to look amazing on film. The challenge was finding a shape and a material that everyone liked.'

Describing that process, Paul recalls, 'It was passed around various sculptors as it went through the different design stages, beginning with quick mock-ups to establish size and shape – as many as fifteen versions – that then got whittled down to three or four before it came back to us and we produced a few more, different treatments.'

Cast in resin and polished, the Arkenstone was the subject of some discussion as to whether it ought to have an internal light source to add a little extra luminosity and a touch of dazzle. 'To be honest,' says Paul, 'we didn't go terribly far with the lighting idea. We looked at LEDs and the option of putting something inside to give it some reflectivity and depth, but we didn't want an Arkenstone with a battery pack. It became really obvious that an approach of that kind was just too fussy, and would turn out to be nowhere near as magical as hoped. Also, as with all props, we needed several identical copies of the Arkenstone and resins tend to be somewhat unpredictable: you may get it right one time but then when trying to repeat it it turns out slightly different. In the end we decided on a simple physical object that could be held in the hand and to leave the magic with which it's imbued to digital post-production.'

ABOVE: *The Arkenstone was enhanced with visual effects to look like it contained a glimpse of the beginning of the universe.*
LEFT: *Bilbo spots something glowing among Smaug's treasure hoard.*

FINDING THE ARKENSTONE

The scene, in the prologue of *An Unexpected Journey*, in which the Arkenstone is first discovered, unexpectedly involved the film's Stunt Co-ordinator, Glenn Boswell, as he explains: 'We were in a meeting about filming the prologue and Casting Department asked if the Dwarf Miner was going to be played by an actor or a stunt double, when Peter suddenly says, "It could be Glenn!" Great! Thanks, Peter! Actually, I was tickled because I knew the Dwarf Miner was the character who discovers the Arkenstone, and that's a big deal in this film. It was also good for me to find out what it was like being inside the Dwarf suits. In fact, it was quite a trying experience: I had to sit on a chair halfway up a rock cliff face, several metres above the floor, chiselling away, looking for jewels. I would zone out and drift off into my own world, trying to keep calm and just get through the day.'

The tedium lifted somewhat when Glenn eventually had to act finding the Arkenstone. 'I got treated like an actor and that was rather fun. They were filming a close-up and they said, "We want you to respond to seeing the stone; your eyes need to be open really wide as if you were thinking 'Wow!'" So, there I am in this cave, covered in prosthetics – including a huge nose – and there's water dripping down on me and running into my eyes and stinging. We shot the scene, over and over, and each time I'd keep getting a message back from Peter asking if I could open my eyes any wider. But my eyes *were* open – *wide* open – and I couldn't open them any wider! And then I hear that Peter is asking, "Why did we pick Glenn? His eyes are too close to his nose!" Thanks again, Peter!'

BURGLAR BAGGINS

W HEN GANDALF ENLISTS – OR, RATHER, COMMANDEERS – BILBO BAGGINS TO ASSIST THORIN AND THE DWARVES WITH THEIR QUEST, HE TELLS THE HOBBIT THAT THE EXPLOIT WILL BE 'VERY AMUSING FOR ME, VERY GOOD FOR YOU – AND PROFITABLE, TOO, VERY LIKELY, IF YOU EVER GET OVER IT.' WHEN TOLKIEN BEGAN HIS STORY, HE NEEDED LITTLE MORE EXPLANATION THAN THAT FOR WHY GANDALF HAD INVOLVED AN UNADVENTUROUS HOBBIT IN AN EXCITING AND POTENTIALLY DANGEROUS ADVENTURE.

Only much later did Tolkien discover that Gandalf had more ambitious motives for encouraging Thorin to reclaim the lost kingdom of Erebor: that of attempting to destroy Smaug before the Dragon could be used by an enemy of the Free Peoples of Middle-earth. A perilous mission with far-reaching consequences was, therefore, relying on the abilities of a seemingly insignificant little character.

Seeking to justify Gandalf's somewhat eccentric choice, Tolkien suggested that hobbits had certain useful qualities such as their ability to move quickly and quietly and, when they wished, remain unobserved. And, as Philippa Boyens explains, Bilbo possessed other useful attributes: 'He's a totally unknown quantity to Smaug because the Dragon has never smelled a hobbit before. He can't quite place

OPPOSITE: *Bilbo doing what hobbits do best: moving stealthily through the Dale ruins.* ABOVE: *Laying low until danger has passed.* BELOW: *Lifting a set of keys from Thranduil's gaoler.*

Bilbo and is, initially, confused and confounded by that. Gandalf may have had another good reason, which was that Bilbo is probably less likely to be overcome by greed than the Dwarves once they see the gold; and, indeed, that turns out to be true.'

However, there is also a very specific reason given to Thorin for taking Bilbo with them and that is that he is a 'burglar'. It is an amusing concept: the respectable Mr Baggins being employed as a thief, but as the filmmakers discovered when turning Tolkien's story into a series of screenplays, it is not immediately clear what burglary Bilbo is supposed to commit.

'The concept of Bilbo as a burglar,' says Peter Jackson, 'is a charmingly funny and quaint idea and there's no doubt that he signed his name to a contract as a burglar before setting out on this journey, but what does it really *mean*? The question confronting us was, quite simply, how do you burgle a Dragon?'

Taking up this question, Philippa asks: 'Is Bilbo meant to steal the treasure, piece by piece? What were they *thinking*? This was a problem that we really needed to address – but one that we needed to address in as close a way as we could to

Bilbo actually being a burglar. The answer, which was established early on, was the Arkenstone.'

'So, in our movie,' says Peter, 'we understand why the Dwarves need a burglar: it's really about wanting him to steal the Arkenstone, which is the mystic heart of the Mountain and the symbol of Thorin's heritage.'

The importance to Thorin and the Dwarves of this ancestral gem becomes not simply a justification for Bilbo's engagement in criminal acts but also crucial to the story as it unfolds in *The Battle of the Five Armies.*

ONE MAN'S JOURNEY

THERE ARE MANY PEOPLE WHO HAVE WORKED ON THE HOBBIT WHO HAVE BEEN ASSOCIATED WITH PETER JACKSON'S FILMMAKING ACROSS MANY YEARS. ONE SUCH INDIVIDUAL IS ACADEMY AWARD-WINNER, CHRISTIAN RIVERS, AND THIS IS HIS STORY…

I was living in Whanganui on the west coast of New Zealand's North Island and was a big horror movie fan in my teens. One day, a friend told me to check out what he referred to as 'a Kiwi gore film': it was called *Bad Taste* and that was the first time I'd heard of its director, Peter Jackson.

When I was sixteen years old, an interest in model-making and special effects led to my visiting the workshop of Wellington art director and production designer, Shayne Radford. He was very frank about the lack of film work in New Zealand, but wished me luck. So I returned to Whanganui and school and carried on watching movies.

After graduating from high school, I didn't really do much other than make a lot of drawings and watch even more movies! Eventually, I began to realize that I'd no prospects and that my life wasn't really going anywhere. About that time I picked up a copy of the American film fan magazine, *Fangoria*, and read an interview with Peter about *Meet the Feebles*. My first thought was, 'I really need to get in contact with this guy.'

I asked for Shayne Radford's help and he said the best person to talk to would be a model-maker called Richard Taylor. Richard was very supportive, so I sent him my entire collection of drawings to date – which was a lot.

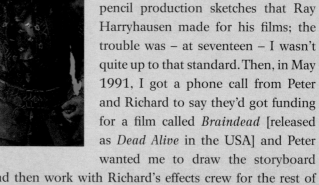

I was gutted when I didn't get a call back immediately, so I rang him. Richard was incredibly complimentary about my work and said he'd shown it to Peter and that he wanted to meet me. I told my Mum and she drove me down to Wellington. The irony of the story is that throughout this time 'P Jackson' was still listed in the Wellington phone book – if I had but looked!

My first 'job' for Peter was some developmental artwork for an absurdly over-the-top fantasy feature film called *Blubberhead* that never got made. I'd do sketches at home and send them down to Peter, but never really nailed what he was after. He would constantly show me beautiful pencil production sketches that Ray Harryhausen made for his films; the trouble was – at seventeen – I wasn't quite up to that standard. Then, in May 1991, I got a phone call from Peter and Richard to say they'd got funding for a film called *Braindead* [released as *Dead Alive* in the USA] and Peter wanted me to draw the storyboard and then work with Richard's effects crew for the rest of the production. I packed my bags and left Whanganui the same week.

Peter always storyboarded his films, so after *Braindead* I did the same job for *Heavenly Creatures*, *The Frighteners* and, later, became the first person to put pencil to paper

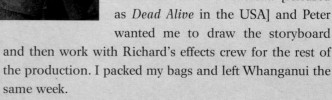

> *I have always loved the energy of being on set, and being in charge of a shooting unit on* The Hobbit *was just awesome – the most fun, memorable and craziest job ever!*

OPPOSITE: *Christian Rivers in action, as Splinter Unit Director inspiring Richard Armitage into battle as Thorin.* ABOVE: *Directing Ian McKellen.* RIGHT: *Working with Peter Jackson and Gaffer Reg Garside.*

for *The Lord of the Rings*. After Universal had scuttled Peter's first attempt to remake *King Kong*, we worked on proposals for several other projects – including one entitled *The Hobbit*! After working at Weta Digital on Robert Zemeckis' *Contact*, I helped Peter begin storyboarding some very early scenes for *The Lord of the Rings*.

Over the years my roles would include Storyboard Artist, Creature Concept Designer, VFX Art Director, Previsualization Supervisor – oh, yes, and a cameo role as a Gondorian Guard! However, the work I enjoyed the most was directing the Splinter Unit for the 2013 pick-ups on *The Hobbit*. My responsibilities were typical of any Second Unit Director working for Peter: get him shots he likes and get him lots of options. It's not your movie, it's his. Thankfully, he's always there to give feedback and help you – which is a great safety net. It's stressful, but it's *good* stress. I have always loved the energy of being on set, and being in charge of a shooting unit on *The Hobbit* was just awesome – the most fun, memorable and craziest job *ever*!

If you were to ask me what the secret of Peter's success is, I'd say he has a childlike love of entertaining cinema that never wanes and he surrounds himself with great people who want to help him achieve his goals. He is also an incredibly shrewd businessman. A lot has changed since we first met: Weta Digital is now one of the largest VFX Facilities in the industry, Stone Street Studios has three massive soundstages and Park Road Post is one of the best Post-Production Facilities in the world. What *hasn't* changed is Peter: he's still the kid at the candy shop. The only difference is that he just has a lot more money to spend on candy and the shop is a lot bigger.

Michael Pellerin, Video Documentary Producer

BEHIND 'BEHIND THE SCENES'

'**I** DON'T HAVE A DEAL YET, I DON'T HAVE A CREW, I DON'T HAVE EQUIPMENT, I DON'T HAVE A BUDGET. I DON'T HAVE ANYTHING! IT WAS JANUARY 2011 AND MICHAEL PELLERIN, IN LOS ANGELES, WAS TAKING A TELEPHONE CALL FROM NEW ZEALAND. PETER JACKSON, HE WAS TOLD, WANTED HIM IN WELLINGTON TO BEGIN SHOOTING BEHIND THE SCENES FOOTAGE OF THE PREPARATIONS FOR THE BEGINNING OF FILMING *THE HOBBIT*. ALTHOUGH MICHAEL KNEW HE WAS LIKELY TO BE WORKING ON THE PROJECT, A SERIES OF DELAYS TO THE PRODUCTION HAD MEANT THAT HE DIDN'T KNOW *WHEN*. SUDDENLY IT WAS ALL SYSTEMS GO, BUT, AS MICHAEL TOLD PRODUCER, ZANE WEINER, HE HAD YET TO BE GIVEN A CONTRACT AND HAD NO RESOURCES. NO PROBLEM, IT SEEMED: 'ZANE SAID, "WE'LL FLY YOU DOWN HERE AND PUT YOU UP IN A HOTEL. PETE WILL LEND YOU HIS CAMERA, AND YOU CAN JUST START SHOOTING."'

And that was the beginning of what, by 2015, will have been four years of documenting the making of *The Hobbit* trilogy. Four years spent helping Peter Jackson create his popular video blogs, avidly followed by fans awaiting the next film release, and the 'Appendices' which make up the bonus features to the Extended Editions of the DVDs.

Fortunately, Michael Pellerin was no stranger to the crazy ways of moviedom, having produced documentary material for many animated films, from Disney classics such as *Snow White and the Seven Dwarfs* to Pixar hits *Toy Story* and *Monsters Inc*. More significantly, he had also already chronicled *The Lord of the Rings* trilogy as well as Peter Jackson's next epic, *King Kong*.

He was well equipped to chart Bilbo's cinematic progress in *The Hobbit*, since he had not only been a devoted fan of Tolkien since his youth but, from a very early age, was passionately in love with film. 'I was fascinated,' he says, 'with the idea of film as a powerful form of public storytelling; that a filmmaker's imagination could create visions which other people could then experience: introducing us to characters and taking us into situations that we would never encounter in real life. Entering these dreamscapes became an obsession for me, which I turned into a career.'

Arriving in Wellington, Michael hired as an assistant a local youngster who was just out of film school and who – having been an Orc extra on *The Return of the King* – was keen to be working on the next Jackson film. With

OPPOSITE: *Dressed in costume as Dori, Mark Hadlow delivers a piece to Meg Parrott, BTS Camera, to be edited into one of the video blogs.* ABOVE: *Michael Pellerin films the filmmaker as Peter frames an extreme close-up of one of the Goblins.*

their borrowed equipment and a borrowed office, the two-man unit – 'We were,' says Michael, 'almost like Robinson Crusoe and Friday!' – began filming the filmmakers.

After a couple of months of exhausting sixteen-hour days, Michael had a team in place including a producer, editors and additional camera crew. The task of reporting the behind-the-scenes exploits of Mr Baggins and Co. was now seriously underway.

As Michael explains, the aim was the same as it had been in covering the making of *The Lord of the Rings*: 'Peter said that he wanted us to tell the story of the project – *warts and all*. What it was *really* like: the challenges, the hardships, the humour and the bizarreness of it all. If we could capture something of that, then it would be real and, if it was real, it would resonate with audiences.'

Michael was acutely aware how privileged he was in getting to see everything that was going on. 'Filming *The Hobbit* involved a series of amazing experiences but only a few of us experienced that journey. A film crew, however big, is still a relatively small number of people in comparison to the world's population. It was our job

❦ You can tell your stories through people's words and memories, recollections and anecdotes, but they will always be stronger if you can tell them visually ❦

to somehow gift the audience the experience of having been there – or, at least, as close as we could.'

In achieving that, Michael and his team benefited from the advice of the film's Director of Photography, Andrew Lesnie: 'Early on he said to me, "Remember, it is a visual medium. You can tell your stories through people's words and memories, recollections and anecdotes, but they will always be stronger if you can tell them visually." That's something we always keep in mind – *think visual*. With Peter's films, he always puts the audience in the middle of the action and we try to do the same: film from the side lines and there's distance between the audience and what's going on, but if the camera is literally right next to Martin Freeman and Peter Jackson having a discussion then the audience is suddenly right there with them.'

That, of course, requires a good deal of quick thinking and tact: 'Everybody on the movie signed on to do their job: to act, create sets, costumes and make-up. They're there to get a film up on the world's cinema screens, but then there's me and my crew, running around making a reality TV show about them making this

movie! So, it's a delicate dance: if you're too cautious and fly-on-the-wall, your audience is never going to be in the centre of the action. But if you get too central, you're likely to get in the way of filming, be a pain in the butt and get yelled at from off-set.'

However, familiarity also has its benefits: 'As a legitimate department of the production, we're part of the team and, being based next door to the production offices, usually the first to know when something's happening. Also, being around every day means we get in people's headlights and before long they are giving us ideas and suggestions: "You really should cover this…" or "It might be fun if you shot that…" And having that input is really valuable and important to the cast and crew because, for them, the documentaries are a sort of time capsule containing their memories of these experiences.'

Covering a mammoth project such as *The Hobbit* places similarly epic demands on the behind-the-scenes team, and whilst they didn't film everything taking place on and around the set, on average they clocked up 3 to 4 hours a day and, at the beginning of 2014, had already shot 18,000 hours, plus 200 hours of interviews.

The significant difference between the two film crews is that one has a script to work to and the other doesn't, as Michael explains: 'Narrative films are written by screenplay writers, but documentaries are written by God! We are story-gatherers; we are permanently watching things develop and asking ourselves, "Is there a story here?" And we're always ready so that if something completely unexpected happens, we're ready to turn on the camera, jump in and grab the moment.'

An example of being in the right place at the right time would be Luke Evans' first day in the role of Bard. 'Luke was a fan of our video blogs,' recalls Michael, 'and, because he joined the project on the second film, he was rather envious of those who had been there since the

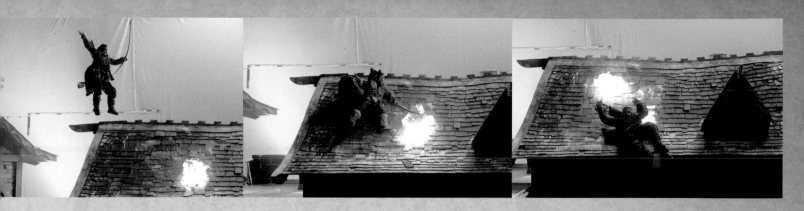

beginning. His first scenes were during Smaug's attack on Lake-town: all day he was leaping and jumping from rooftop to rooftop, firing arrows and fighting, coping with incredibly elaborate stunt work. Peter certainly put him through his paces!'

No wonder then, when Michael later interviewed Luke, the actor confessed that it was the hardest, most demanding and physically exhausting day's work he had ever done on a movie. 'Most of the time,' says Michael, 'when you ask an actor what was their toughest day and they tell you, you're unable to show it, but because we are so embedded in the production and were there with the crew, we had the footage of his ordeal. Instead of just having Luke as a talking head, we could show exactly what he was talking *about*!'

Another instance would be the day on location in the Rock and Pillar Range, the rugged landscape near Strath Taieri in the South Island. The Dwarves were trekking across the wild, rocky terrain towards the Desolation of Smaug. 'The scenery,' says Michael, 'looks like an alien planet and the only way to get the cast and crew up there was via a huge helicopter migration. So, we're filming up there and, all of a sudden, clouds start closing in until we were literally on this weird, mountainous island above the clouds.'

Anxiety quickly set in with the realization that filming had to be abandoned and everyone had to be got to safety while it was still possible to fly the helicopters. 'We all knew that, at some point, it would become unsafe to travel, and Peter and the whole cast and crew would be stranded on this desolate mountaintop for the night. So, they start the evacuation, but even though we've got a lot of helicopters the number of people involved means that there have to be many, many rounds of flights to get everybody off.'

With time running out, and visibility failing, it was decided to leave the equipment overnight, and concentrate on the personnel. 'The final group,' remembers Michael, 'didn't make the last helicopter to fly and had to walk off the mountain. But guess what? We were there and filmed the whole adventure, and were there to film the last of the party as they eventually hiked back into camp. An amazing experience, but you had to have been there, and if we *hadn't* been there, it would simply have been a story that people told but which the audience would never see.'

Reflecting on his work behind the scenes, Michael Pellerin says: 'I am my own audience. I never try to second-guess what the audience is going to want. I assume that people who watch our work love these movies and are going to be fascinated to find out more about them. So, it's my job to tell the most entertaining, interesting, compelling stories possible. Ultimately I make these films to please myself and, hopefully, if we do our job well enough, then the chances are we might also please an audience. If not, then I need to find another job!'

TOP: *Luke Evans' first day on set was captured by the Behind the Scenes crew.* LEFT: *The storm clouds gather at Strath Taieri behind the oblivious actors.* RIGHT: *Michael Pellerin prepares to get the perfect shot regardless of storms.*

BEHIND 'BEHIND THE SCENES'

> *I think Fili, especially, feels that weight of responsibility of what potentially he may become. He is the older one so he feels protective of his younger brother*

Battle Plans – The General's View

THE BATTLE OF THE FIVE ARMIES, LIKE ALL THE OTHER SKIRMISHES, SIEGES AND FULL-ON WARFARE IN *THE LORD OF THE RINGS* AND *THE HOBBIT*, TAKES PLACE UNDER THE SUPREME COMMAND OF PETER JACKSON, WHO HERE REFLECTS ON THE NATURE OF THIS CONFRONTATION:

For the Battle of the Five Armies, we're following very much the mantra of *The Lord of the Rings*, in that we're not just showing endless shots of nameless Dwarves, Elves, Men and Orcs fighting and fighting. My aim is always for us not to go for more than a couple of shots without seeing one of our principals in action, because the battle is just a backdrop against which we can follow the many individual storylines – some of which have been in play since the first film – until each reaches its climactic moment amongst the chaos of the battlefield.

In essence, the Battle of the Five Armies is a fight for dominance of the Dwarven lands. It's almost as if Sauron were making his opening move, his first play, in the vast Middle-earth-wide chess game that he's undertaking. It's the beginnings of the War of the Ring that will only ultimately be resolved in the final battle of *The Return of the King*. In twentieth-century terms, it's the equivalent of Germany's invasion of Poland, which led to the Second World War.

What I really like about this movie is all the characters that come together on the Lonely Mountain come with

very different agendas. There are the Dwarves who just want to recover their homeland – who can blame them? – and to do that they first have to drive out Smaug. But, having done that, Thorin and the Dwarves are holed up in the Lonely Mountain with their long-desired ancestral wealth, and with Thorin increasingly succumbing to the Dragon sickness that causes him to cling ruthlessly to his gold and to defend it against all-comers.

There is Bard and the people of Lake-town, whose city has been destroyed, who request the help of the Dwarves of Erebor. Their motivation isn't greed but simply the need to survive. Then there is Thranduil, who comes with his own motivations and demands fired by an age-old vendetta with Thorin's grandfather, Thror. Meanwhile, a vast Dwarven army led by Dáin Ironfoot is marching from the Iron Hills of the East to Thorin's aid. Everyone's operating from different agendas and clashing with one another, which, for a filmmaker, is always more fun than just having good characters fighting bad ones. Those going into battle against one another include characters – Elves, Men and Dwarves – that, as an audience, we like regardless of which side they are on.

But then there is also the common enemy that will, eventually, drive the warring factions to unite: two massive attacking forces of Orcs. There's the army that Gandalf has seen mustering at Dol Guldur led by Azog and another that Legolas and Tauriel witness marching south from Gundabad under the command of Bolg. The Orcs have a different agenda again: they're not coming for gold; they're coming because their ultimate leader, the Necromancer – who, as Gandalf has realized, is none other than Sauron – doesn't want the Dwarves to re-establish their kingdom. All the time Smaug was living in the Lonely Mountain the Necromancer was content, because the Dragon was, in a way, looking after things for him. Fearful that, without the Dragon's help, the Dwarves will become a mighty force once more, the Necromancer knows that now is the time to strike.

And this is where Gandalf's story weaves in with everyone else's, for he is having to deal with the potential return of Sauron and is trying to prevent the Dark Power taking over Middle-earth again. However, the outcome can, at best, only be a fragile resolution and one that he cannot hope will last forever: it is like putting a tiny Band Aid on a major wound; underneath, something remains that will, eventually, begin to fester and that will be a problem that Gandalf will have to face and deal with in sixty years' time as told *in The Lord of the Rings*.

Fortunes of War: The Battle of the Five Armies

'THE BATTLE OF THE FIVE ARMIES IS GOING TO MAKE THE BATTLE OF THE PELENNOR FIELDS LOOK LIKE A VILLAGE CRICKET MATCH!' THAT'S JOHN HOWE'S TAKE ON THE CONFRONTATION THAT WILL BRING THE STORY OF *THE HOBBIT* TO ITS ACTION-PACKED CLIMAX.

At the time this book was being readied for printing, the combined creative armies of Weta Workshop and Weta Digital were still involved in finalizing their battle tactics, but – between briefing their forces – their leaders took time out to provide a few insights into the conflict which lies ahead of them.

'These films,' says Weta Workshop's Richard Taylor, 'and in particular the third, are the most challenging task we've ever undertaken at our design studio. You might think, coming to *The Hobbit* after *The Lord of the Rings*, that we would require significant less design, but Peter was absolutely focused on never giving the audience the feeling that we were just resting on our laurels, that we'd done it before and that all we had to do was show you the same again. And the same applies to the battles.'

What distinguishes the climactic battle in *The Hobbit* from those in the *Rings* trilogy is the size and intricacy of the engagement, as Richard explains: 'We all aspire for it to be the greatest battle that's been seen on screen: five incredible, powerful forces coming together on a single battlefield, fighting over an unbelievably complex terrain, where the different armies will each benefit from the land-scapes best suited to their physicality and capabilities.'

Weta Digital's Joe Letteri agrees: 'The battle takes place over several different locations – outside the gate to Erebor, in Dale, up at Ravenhill – and massing on that battlefield will be multiple armies, each of which not only

OPPOSITE, LEFT TO RIGHT: *Thranduil, protected by his black armour, appears cool in the heat of battle; Richard Taylor helps Richard Armitage into the golden armour of Thorin's grandfather, Thrór.* ABOVE: *The Necromancer's Orc army marches to war.* BELOW: *Thranduil's map of the Lonely Mountain is laid out to help plan the battle ahead* (left); *Richard Armitage wields Orcrist again under Peter's direction* (right).

needs to be stylistically unique but has the look of belonging to Middle-earth while, at the same time, being something that we have not seen before.'

Defining how the Battle of the Five Armies will differ from previous offensives, Joe says: 'Many of our earlier battles – such as Helm's Deep and Minas Tirith – were more or less sieges, whereas here the armies are going to be clashing in the open. We have had a sense of that type of warfare in the various prologues that we've done for *Rings* and for the first *Hobbit* film, but they were sort of told in vignettes. Now we're going to stage a battle where audiences need to understand the strategy in order to be able to grasp what's at stake and to follow what happens as the battle ebbs and flows.'

This particular battle will involve creatures and war machines that will be wholly new to fans of Jackson's Middle-earth. 'What's more,' says, Joe: 'when it comes to the creatures that you might expect to see we want them to look as far from the ordinary as possible. Essentially, everything is being given its own unique design.'

It is an aspiration shared by Richard Taylor, who offers a characteristic description of Weta Workshop's contribution to the war effort: 'It's been an absolute playground for the likes of our minds, designing an unbelievable array of amazing creatures, war machines, and fighting styles for

CLOCKWISE, FROM TOP LEFT: *Gandalf enters the fray; stunt crew dressed as Gundabad Orcs march on to set; Bolg wields a huge mace that resembles a spinal column; Orlando Bloom rehearses firing past Peter's beard; the Dwarves prepare for battle; Aidan Turner as Kili with looks to die for; and Oin reviews the Erebor armoury.*

the various combatants. We have, for example, an Elven army riding in to fight alongside a Dwarven army: and that alliance alone is just one of the many intriguing complexities to the telling of this story.'

The diversity of creatures being employed on the battlefield is staggering, as Richard explains: 'We have Dwarves on huge armoured boars and others on battle-machine chariots, pulled by armoured mountain goats. There are burrowing creatures – serpent-like worms, giant shrews and moles – that might tunnel under the attacking army and come up in the middle of their forces; and great war-Trolls specifically trained – and, in some cases, maimed – in order to make them more insane and effective in battle.'

Turning to the topic of armour and weapons, Richard says: 'I've always wanted to be able to make some medieval-style armour designed to turn humans into what look like small battle tanks. And indeed that is exactly what we have done in dressing the Dwarves in elaborate – almost architecturally fortified – suits of armour with their huge beards but little else showing through the steel plates.'

In sharp contrast to all this hardware is the military force of Lake-town, as Richard explains: 'They have a minimal standing militia, it's more of a home guard for the master's wealth, so when they were called to arms we equipped them with a tin-pot collection of one-off home-made weaponry including fishing spears, gutting knives strapped onto long poles, anchors and nets, bows made out of reeds lashed together and basketware turned into shields and body protection.'

In arming the Orcs, says Richard, Weta took their initial inspiration from the director: 'Instead of a rabble such as those serving Sauron in *Rings*, Peter wanted them to be a daunting, disciplined and highly intelligent fighting force. For them we devised some of the most hideous and bizarre weaponry that we've created to date: vicious-looking, crude in construction but incredibly efficient in its use. Peter also wanted us to steer clear of metal plate armour so they are protected by formidable-looking armour in aggressively iconic shapes whilst being made from little more than fabric and bone.' With a laugh he adds, 'And *that* is just one of the many challenges we faced in preparing for the Battle of the Five Armies!'

PETER JACKSON ON THORIN & ARMITAGE

Talking about the character of Thorin when he first began filming *The Hobbit*, Richard Armitage likened the part to that of Macbeth or one of Shakespeare's other tragic monarchs. Here Peter Jackson talks about the role and the actor:

Thorin is a wonderful character and I think people will understand just how brilliant Richard Armitage is in the role when they see his performance in *The Battle of the Five Armies*. In the final part of the trilogy, Richard has to take Thorin to the brink of utter madness and then bring him back from that point to a heroic place again.

Across the three films, Richard runs the full gamut from being utterly despicable to being somebody for whom you feel such affection that you will be prepared to shed tears for him. He plays the part very truthfully – he doesn't play madness like a hammy Shakespearean actor doing *Richard III*, and, as a result, it is a triumph of acting.

Richard keeps Thorin's temporary insanity internalized, which is ultimately scarier than more extroverted demonstrations of madness. The nutcases that rant and rave are never as terrifying as the silent, brooding, quietly stewing guys, the ones in whom the emotional pressure is eroding them away from within.

This final movie has a lot more tension than the previous films: almost from the beginning until virtually the very end, everything for Thorin – and for all the characters – is very much poised on a knife edge which, for a filmmaker, is an immensely satisfying mood to be creating.

THE SOUNDS OF VIOLENCE

ACROSS THE VAST SPAN OF TOLKIEN'S HISTORY OF MIDDLE-EARTH THERE ARE AS MANY ACCOUNTS OF BATTLES AND WARS AS CAN BE FOUND IN THE HISTORY OF OUR OWN WORLD, AND FILMING THESE CONFLICTS BRINGS MANY CHALLENGES, NOT LEAST IN FINDING WAYS TO CAPTURE THE CLASH AND ROAR OF THE BATTLEFIELD. SOUND DESIGNER, DAVE WHITEHEAD, REVEALS SOME OF THEIR SOUND TACTICS.

'Most of the sounds you hear on the soundtrack of any movie are not those that were audible when the scene was being filmed but have been recorded and created later to fit the precise moment and help tell the story by making what is seen on screen *sound* as convincing as it *looks*.'

It is rare, as Dave explains, for any sounds that are eventually used to be in their raw recorded form: 'Most recordings will undergo some form of surgery to transform them into a usable sound-effect as, for example, when we record outside and there's the background murmur of city life which would make them unusable in a period fantasy film. Fortunately, we now have software that can help us analyze any recorded sound and, if necessary, remove the parts of it that we don't want – including wind and even birdsong. A recording can easily be marred by a blackbird singing all through it, but now we can simply remove the songster.'

When it comes to creating noise of battle, what you hear is invariably a combination of a number of different sounds. 'A single sword hit,' says Dave, 'can have various

OPPOSITE: *Now wielding two swords, Lee Pace ensures that Thranduil is a whirling dervish on the battlefield.* RIGHT: *Bombur prepares to blow his horn, one of the final Hobbit props to be made by Weta Workshop.* BELOW: *The makeshift materials with which the Lake-town refugees arm themselves provided the Sound team with interesting opportunities for a sound palette.*

layers to give it movement, weight, elegance and to make the person who wields the sword sound like they mean business. For a sword-fight you have *whoosh*es or *swish*es for the incoming sword and general movement of the weapon. Then, you have the sound of impact. Are they striking another sword, or armour, or are they hitting flesh? You have to layer sounds to cover both the sword and the object that's being hit. Every action has a reaction and combining the two is what gives colour to the soundscape.'

Many of the recordings used are drawn from an already existing library of sound effects, as Dave explains: 'Over the years of working on *Rings*, the team have built up an extensive library of recorded and designed sounds for battle sequences which have provided an invaluable starting point for researching the kind of battlescapes in *The Hobbit*.'

Many other sounds, however, will be custom built: different types of metal of various weights and sizes are suspended and recordings are made of them being hit and struck in different ways and with varying intensity – everything from a light, glancing clash to a heavy full-on blow. Every weapon dictates its own sound, as Dave describes: 'The Elven swords have slick swishes and a resonance which is very elegant-sounding. Supervising Sound Editor, Brent Burge, wanted them to have a ninja-like sound that he described as "a steely threat – an almost silent slice". Eventually, Sound Effects Editor, Hayden Collow, successfully captured this elusive sound by recording a very thin blade and it was added to what we call the "*whoosh*" element: that aural quality that adds a real sense of urgency to the sword moves. The sound of the Elven swords is the dramatic opposite of the dull and rusty sound of the Orcs' iron weapons which have a more distorted and discordant resonance.'

There is, of course, a world of difference between a skirmish with a small band of Orcs and a major battleground sequence with massed armies and individual scenes of combat being played against a background of a general melee. 'The key to a good battle,' says Dave, 'is a carefully tailored background battle and a sharply focused foreground. If you are designing or editing sounds for a battle sequence you have to set limits on how much detail you will create or leave in. Have everything on the screen making a noise and you have a cacophony. Of course, on a real battlefield there wouldn't be any sort of order, but on screen it would be all too easy for scenes such as the Battle of Azanulbizar at Moria in *An Unexpected Journey* or the Battle of the Five Armies to become nothing but a chaotic aural soup. Our job is to guide the audience into what action to follow – which is usually pretty obvious as the film is generally shot that way – and we do that by editing the foreground layer or "hero moves", as we call them, and the background layer.'

♦ Over the years of working on Rings, *the team have built up an extensive library of recorded and designed sounds for battle sequences which have provided an invaluable starting point for researching the kind of battlescapes in* The Hobbit *♦*

Differentiating between those two extremes, Dave says: 'The background layers are of varying intensities, depending on the type of battle and location, and are made up of various components. Get it right and you can give dynamic sweeping shape to the battle before adding the sounds of the "hero" battle. The foreground is what the audience will be most focused on and doesn't often exceed more than three simultaneous skirmishes because we can only take in so much. It's good to focus on one fight and make it great

and then do any major moves either side of it. Again, you have to keep it simple or the audience will be swamped with sounds and it will find it overwhelming.

The full complexity of the Sound Department's contribution becomes clear when you consider the work that goes into creating the various layers that will make up the background soundscape, against which our heroes and their enemies struggle for supremacy. Here is the Dave Whitehead Guide to good battle backgrounds:

General Battle-rumble: 'This is to cover foot and body movement for a mass of characters or creatures. When working on *The Lord of the Rings*, we recorded two hundred soldiers from the New Zealand Army having mock battles, marching, breathing and chanting. This has been a great source for helping build these battle rumbles. You can also use unlikely sources like car tyres driving on gravel: pitched down, this can sound like an army or mounted soldiers rumbling over a hill.'

Armour: 'We are very fortunate to have medieval re-enactment groups all over New Zealand and they have been a great source for getting the sound of armoured groups on the move. Otherwise, we literally gather every piece of armour available and have as many people as we can muster moving vigorously or running around microphones to capture an isolated armour sound.'

Weapons: 'This is usually designed and made from many recordings and tends to be a bright metallic, almost tinkly, layer. As with the armour, we have recorded mock-sword battles several times, where people stand around the microphones and hit sword against sword. We also record many individual swords, metal objects and other weapons in the studio. I have bought plenty of swords in the past for various films but Weta are always kind enough to lend us real weapons and props.'

Vocals: 'We will create non-specific background vocal activity to suggest the people and creatures involved in the conflict. We refer to these as "walla" tracks and they comprise a combination of treated human vocals and animal roars and cries.'

Every confrontation makes its own unique demands: 'The Battle of Azanulbizar,' recalls Dave, 'was depicted as a flashback in the first film and Peter wanted the sequence to be very ethereal or dream-like in nature, as if it were a battle seen from the perspective of memory. The overall sound was created through sweeping layers of Orc vocals and battle movement and, although Azog and Thorin were the key focus of this scene, Peter wanted even them to have a washed-out or echoey feel.'

In contrast were the complex sounds created for the running battle between the Dwarves and the Goblins in the labyrinthine caverns beneath the Misty Mountains. 'The action on screen,' says Dave, 'was underscored with waves of screeching Goblin vocals, played through a genuine cave acoustic, together with the sound of them swarming over the rocks and precarious wooden walkways. We found the perfect place to record the sound of Goblins running on the set for Lake-town, which was full of wooden catwalks and jetties.

In our diligence, we decided we'd record ourselves running about with bare feet, on these wooden walkways, on a deserted film set – at night! Music Editor, Steve Gallagher, joined us for the recording session and we enthusiastically rushed around. Unfortunately, Steve encountered a jutting piece of wood and broke his toe! So, in honour of his noble efforts to help us, his agonized scream of pain is now forever immortalized in the film!'

THIS PAGE: *The sound of battle is a combination of noises, with carefully balanced layers of foreground and background sounds.*

BOWS & ARROWS

Any battle in *The Hobbit* is going to involve archery, and with several fabled archers among the characters the sounds made by their bows and arrows were a major component in various fight and battle scenes, as Supervising Sound Editor, Brent Burge, explains: 'Bows are like swords in that they assume the character of the archer: Orc bows, for example, have a chunky barely-held-together release sound with a coarse, uneven arrow flight. Elven bows, on the other hand, are much finer in quality. I made Legolas' bow based on the same elements I used for *Rings* and it has the Legolas signature. Bard's bow gave us the opportunity to develop a powerful new weapon, the sound of which needs to evoke a precision instrument in the hands of a legendary bowman.'

Authentic bow and arrow sounds are, however, among the most elusive to record: 'In real life,' says Brent, 'bow releases and arrow flights are very quiet, but they *do* have a distinct sound which we attempted to capture – with as much variety as we could – in our recordings. Since there's only so much background noise you can remove from an already quite quiet sound we tried to do this in as near-silent an environment as we could find. The problem, however, was finding somewhere where sounds were minimal but which had enough length to cope with an arrow release.

'We were fortunate to have access to the K (or "Kong") Sound Stage at the Studios before they vacated the Lot. This huge sound-proofed shooting stage was perfect for our requirements and we recorded Sound Designer, Dave Whitehead, shooting arrows and the associated sounds of the arrows travelling and making impact.

'The bow release was recorded from various perspectives and at a distance from the targets so as to give us lots of separation from the sounds of the hit. We placed microphones along the line of travel to record the sound of the arrow as it left the bow, passed by and approached the target. For the impacts we assembled targets of different materials in order to give lots of variation. We discovered, for instance, that arrows shot into the trunk of a native New Zealand fern gave us a fantastic crunchy flesh-impact sound. As well as hits we also recorded arrows ricocheting off the targets and clattering onto the ground.

'The arrows themselves were modified by attaching appendages to create variations in the sound of their travel. These included quarter-inch tape, whistles, table tennis balls — you name it, we tried it! A surprising number were successful although, inevitably, it was, you might say, a bit "hit and miss".'

THE UNEXPECTED TRIANGLE: TAURIEL, KILI & LEGOLAS

'*THE HOBBIT*,' SAYS PHILIPPA BOYENS, 'IS A VERY BLOKEY STORY! ALTHOUGH PROFESSOR TOLKIEN WROTE SOME WONDERFUL FEMALE CHARACTERS, YOU ARE VERY AWARE OF THE LACK OF THEM IN THIS BOOK.'

Agreeing, Peter Jackson comments: 'We really weren't comfortable with that situation, feeling that there were opportunities here that were being missed.'

A partial solution was the reintroduction of Galadriel (who, as the screenwriters are the first to admit, is a character not found within the pages of *The Hobbit*) but there was still a wish to find another female role. It was this requirement that eventually resulted in the creation of a 'new' character, Tauriel the Sylvan Elf, although several other options were considered before turning to the Elven kingdom of Mirkwood.

Philippa Boyens recalls: 'We asked ourselves what opportunities might allow for the adding of a good, strong, female character who could have her own story. We didn't just want to create her for the sake of it; she needed to have a purpose in the storytelling, so we looked at a few interesting places where that could happen. Could she be a hobbit, such as Frodo's mother, Primula? Unfortunately, she offered us little opportunity to continue her story outside the Shire and we wanted a character who had her own reason for being in the narrative.'

The writers examined other possibilities, as Peter explains: 'We thought about having a character in Lake-town, but the idea that, as screenwriters, interested us the most and that we thought we could explore and take in directions that would be interesting was the idea of a female Elven character. Fran and I always loved the little thread in *The Lord of the Rings* storyline about the devotion of Gimli – a rough, doughty Dwarf – for the Lady Galadriel. There was something about that story of a love that could never be, that spoke to the idea that you can find attraction anywhere and it can be surprising.'

LEFT: *In pursuit of their foe, Evangeline Lilly and Orlando Bloom as Tauriel and Legolas discuss the best way forward.*
RIGHT: *A troubled Tauriel considers her future.*

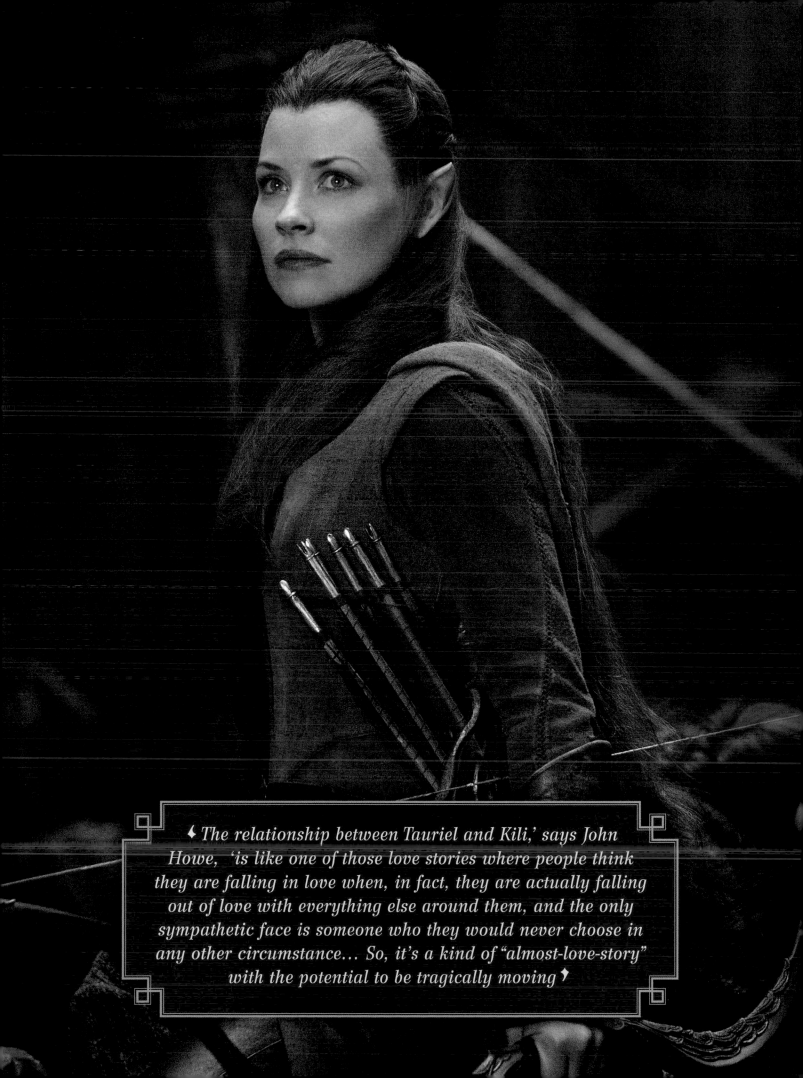

'The relationship between Tauriel and Kili,' says John Howe, 'is like one of those love stories where people think they are falling in love when, in fact, they are actually falling out of love with everything else around them, and the only sympathetic face is someone who they would never choose in any other circumstance... So, it's a kind of "almost-love-story" with the potential to be tragically moving'

ABOVE: *Legolas is caught between his duty to his father, Thranduil, and his concern for his friend, Tauriel.* BELOW: *Kili's rune stone given to him by his mother, Dís.*

The idea developed into a plot-line featuring a love-story between Tauriel and Kili the Dwarf. 'Because of the rancour and animosity existing between the two races,' says Philippa, 'it was an idea that was too tempting to ignore and not so out-landish to be impossible. In the cul-ture of Middle-earth it is historical, rather than natural, for Dwarves and Elves to hate each other. We wanted to show that if you leave two young people alone, they will find common interests and shared expe-riences, so that's what we did.'

Explaining Tauriel's role as one of Thranduil's guards, Peter Jackson says: 'She's a soldier and, as such, is as deadly as Legolas, but at the same time we didn't want to turn her into Xena: Warrior Princess. We wanted her to be more interesting and complex than merely some-one who fights. She's protecting this kingdom ruled by an isolationist, but she has a great curiosity about the outside world. She wants to see mountains, lakes and rivers, and things she's heard about in the history, stories and poetry of the Elves. That, we thought, would give us interesting places to go with her character.'

Add into this situation Thranduil's son, Legolas (still sixty years before forging his friendship with Gimli), and as Peter explains, interesting undercurrents are created: 'Legolas is caught between Thranduil and Tauriel. He totally respects his father who is everything to him, but, at the same time he and Tauriel have grown up together and been friends for a long time. Legolas can see her pain and longing and wants to help her while not betraying his father. And that provided us with a sit-uation in which we could weave some interesting story dynamics.'

THE OFFICIAL MOVIE GUIDE

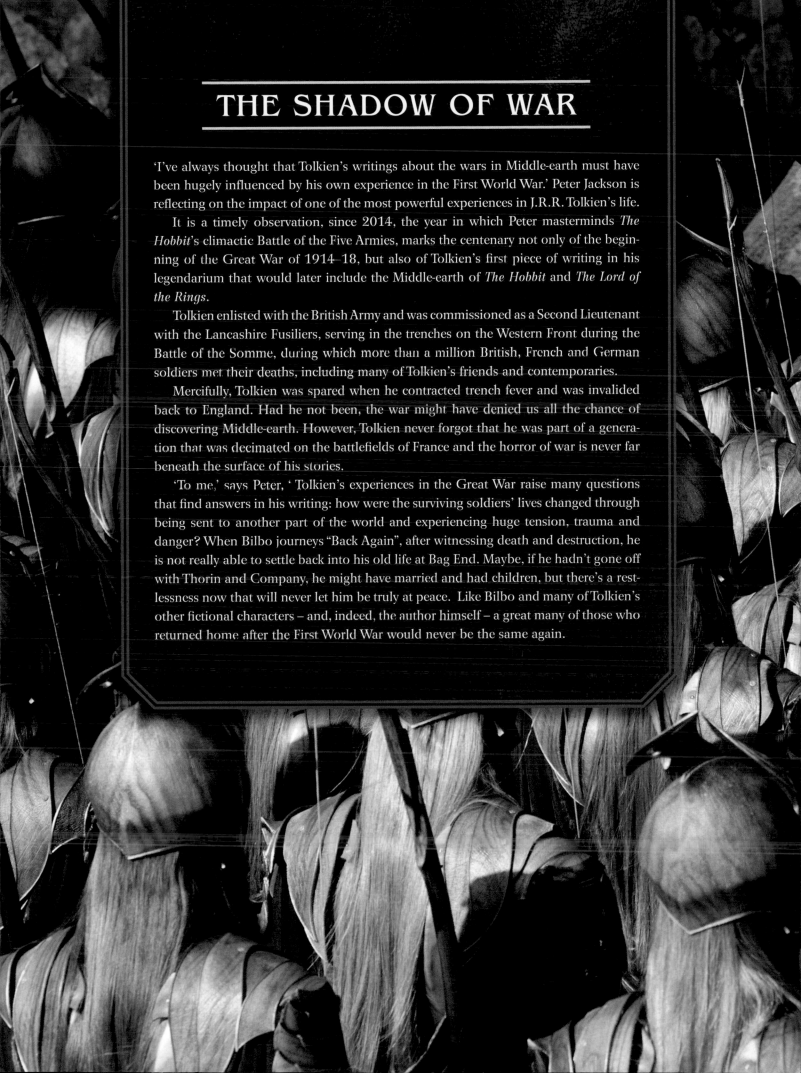

THE SHADOW OF WAR

'I've always thought that Tolkien's writings about the wars in Middle-earth must have been hugely influenced by his own experience in the First World War.' Peter Jackson is reflecting on the impact of one of the most powerful experiences in J.R.R. Tolkien's life.

It is a timely observation, since 2014, the year in which Peter masterminds *The Hobbit*'s climactic Battle of the Five Armies, marks the centenary not only of the beginning of the Great War of 1914–18, but also of Tolkien's first piece of writing in his legendarium that would later include the Middle-earth of *The Hobbit* and *The Lord of the Rings*.

Tolkien enlisted with the British Army and was commissioned as a Second Lieutenant with the Lancashire Fusiliers, serving in the trenches on the Western Front during the Battle of the Somme, during which more than a million British, French and German soldiers met their deaths, including many of Tolkien's friends and contemporaries.

Mercifully, Tolkien was spared when he contracted trench fever and was invalided back to England. Had he not been, the war might have denied us all the chance of discovering Middle-earth. However, Tolkien never forgot that he was part of a generation that was decimated on the battlefields of France and the horror of war is never far beneath the surface of his stories.

'To me,' says Peter, ' Tolkien's experiences in the Great War raise many questions that find answers in his writing: how were the surviving soldiers' lives changed through being sent to another part of the world and experiencing huge tension, trauma and danger? When Bilbo journeys "Back Again", after witnessing death and destruction, he is not really able to settle back into his old life at Bag End. Maybe, if he hadn't gone off with Thorin and Company, he might have married and had children, but there's a restlessness now that will never let him be truly at peace. Like Bilbo and many of Tolkien's other fictional characters – and, indeed, the author himself – a great many of those who returned home after the First World War would never be the same again.

> *Kili is a more audacious kind of guy; he's up for fun and he's up for smashing a few heads. Thorin is someone who they aspire to be like and somebody that they really want to impress, and what better time than now?*

THIS PAGE: *Early concept art by John Howe of Dáin complete with his tusked beard; (inset) Bob Buck's costume design revealing the Dwarf Lord in all his finery.* OPPOSITE: *Billy Connolly.*

Billy Connolly
DÁIN IRONFOOT

'I'M A KING DWARF,' BILLY CONNOLLY TOLD A JOURNALIST ON JOINING THE CAST OF *THE HOBBIT*. 'HE'S A REAL BADASS – RIDES A PIG AND KILLS PEOPLE WITH AN AXE. I LOVE HIM!'

The Dwarf in question is Dáin II, known as 'Ironfoot', a second cousin of Thorin Oakenshield who rules the Dwarves of the Iron Hills in Wilderland and who aids Thorin and Company in their Quest to recover the Dwarven kingdom of Erebor.

Describing his character in greater detail, Billy says, 'He has tattoos on his forehead and cheeks, a big scar down the left side of his face from previous battles, and a broken nose. He's been around a long time and knows the tricks, but he's also been through the mill – like one of those boxers who's slightly overweight and about two or three steps down the bill from the championship fights. He's gone a few rounds, is still in the game and doesn't mind a smack in the mouth from time to time.'

Although *The Desolation of Smaug* marks Billy's Middle-earth debut, the Scottish actor, comedian and musician was originally considered for the role of Gimli when *The Lord of the Rings* was being cast. Best known for his BAFTA-nominated role as the highland ghillie in the royal service of Judi Dench's Queen Victoria in *Mrs Brown*, he has appeared in many films, including *Muppet Treasure Island*, *The Man Who Sued God*, *The Last Samurai*, *Lemony Snicket's A Series of Unfortunate Events* and *Gulliver's Travels*, as well as providing character voices in Disney's *Pocahontas* and Pixar's *Brave*.

Billy recalls how he came to receive the invitation to play the part: 'They said it was only a cameo role, small but important. The character's name appealed to me right away, because "Dáin Ironfoot" sounded real hard:

this guy who suddenly comes out of the darkness – "Oh, no, it's *him*!" – and everyone's quite in awe of this mean, axe-carrying swine, who likes being leader and killing people. I grew up in Glasgow and Dáin appealed to the Glaswegian in me! I couldn't wait to play him.'

Something else about the project piqued the actor's curiosity: 'The bit I really liked,' he laughs, 'was that I was sent a page of dialogue and my character wasn't on it – didn't figure at all – so I thought, "Well, *that's* interesting!" And it got more interesting when I arrived in New Zealand and they gave me a whole script that turned out to be for the *first* movie – which I wasn't going to be in! "Well, well," I'm thinking, "they work pretty weird here!" But, of course, Peter Jackson's reputation goes before him; I had only to look at the standard of his films to know that it would be amazing just to be part of it.'

Not that the actor could even remotely be described as a fan of Tolkien's book, as he recalls with some amusement: 'Peter asked me for lunch on the first day and asked if I'd read *The Hobbit*. "No," I replied, "not only haven't I read it, I don't like people who have." You see, before I did comedy I came from a folk music, bluegrass background. And back then in the hippy sixties there were two distinct camps: the "Tolkiens" and "non-Tolkiens" and I was definitely a "non"! I didn't like the Tolkien people – running around with this book under their arm, talking about Glippity-Globbles and Bibbity-Bobbles. I used to think, "Oh, bugger off!" I know it sounds glib, but I've never read the book of a movie that I'm going to be in, and I've been in several. Sometimes people say, "Oh, I saw the movie, it was nothing like the book." Well, it's not *supposed* to be: a book's a book and a movie's a movie and, with *The Hobbit*, I was in New Zealand to make a movie not a book.'

Few of Billy Connolly's previous roles have been quite as scene-stealing as the red-headed Dáin. Whilst the make-up is designed to create the illusion that the almost six-foot tall actor has the physical proportions of a Dwarf, the character has his own unique features: 'I've got fiery red hair that goes right down my back, a huge red beard embellished with bling that they hook onto my own beard and that reaches to my waist. And anyone who knows me will notice that my moustache is much longer than usual because there's another one attached to it that hangs down like a pair of tusks. In fact, Martin Freeman said it was like acting with a buffalo!'

For Billy, one of the most surprising features of his make-over was the experience of putting on his prosthetic hands: 'They are three times the size of my own hands and I thought, "God, they look awfully false," but they were in total proportion to the rest of my new body; so when they took them off and I looked in the mirror I had these wee funky hands and looked deformed!'

As well as the hands, there's the jewellery: 'I've big fat rings for my big fat fingers. One of them is of a boar's head, which I'm dying to steal. It just has that quality about it that says, "Steal me, steal me!" Except, of course, that it would be of no use to me because it's big enough to fit on my wrist.'

Like Thorin and his Company, Billy had to learn the 'ancient art' of walking like a Dwarf: 'We've got a low-slung centre of gravity, us Dwarves, so when we walk we have to drop our stomachs, so I practiced and practiced

walking with my belly sticking out for days. But then, as soon as I put the costume on – which was like wearing a piano covered in velvet – the weight was so great that I could hardly walk and it turned out I actually hadn't needed to practice at all!'

It was a situation that took the actor only a short while to overcome: 'When I first got a glimpse of myself, I thought, "What am I going to do?" And then I wandered over and I looked at myself in a full-length mirror and an immediate spring came into my step because I realized, "This guy is terrifying!" You'd think he's going to bite you in the face. And he *would*, given half a chance – if there wasn't a possibility that it might spoil his beard bling.'

Billy is particularly keen on the way he makes his first appearance in the film, riding directly towards the Elven army on his wild boar. 'It's a real baddie, black-hat entrance. They're standing still, in formation, but I just keep coming towards them, until they figure out I'm going nowhere else and they part and I ride between their lines, looking at them with great scorn.'

Dáin's attitude towards Elves is uncompromising: 'He hates most people, really. He likes Dwarves and it pretty much ends there. He has absolutely no time for Elves: an angelic bunch of "Jersey Boys", airy-fairy, fancy men with their long blond, braided hair, swishy swords, tra-la-la-la and all that. Of course, Dáin also takes a bit of time over his appearance, but whereas Elves dress to look to great, he dresses to look terrifying. That's the difference.'

Belying his seventy years, Billy Connolly prepared for the Battle of the Five Armies by training with Swordmaster, Steve McMichael: 'I did an hour-and-a-half, three days a week, every week. It was really intensive and you feel that everybody's great at it – except you. But whenever you think you're not making any progress, Steve kindly reminds you of just what a dork you were when you first

❦ … when we walk we have to drop our stomachs, so I practiced and practiced walking with my belly sticking out for days. But then, as soon as I put the costume on – which was like wearing a piano covered in velvet – the weight was so great that I could hardly walk and it turned out I actually hadn't needed to practice at all! ❧

arrived. Steve delights in teaching violence and he'll tell you how to behead somebody with great *joie de vivre*.'

Dáin's weapon of choice is the double-headed axe, as Billy explains: 'The shaft's about five foot long and the blade's curved like a scimitar for slicing into people. On the other end of the shaft is a ball with spikes sticking out of it, like a hedgehog, for stabbing people in the face. So I can hit you with the blade and then get you on the way back with the hedgehog. It's beautifully made but is really quite an alarming piece of equipment.'

Billy's initial approach to battle tactics owed something to another equally competitive activity: 'I would swing my axe and my legs would kind of cross, the way a golfer's do when he swings a club. Well, that's something you really mustn't do! In order to get the brute force that you need, your legs must remain slightly apart with your feet facing the same way, because you're not swinging it all the way like a golfer on account of the fact that there's an enemy body somewhere in between the beginning and the end of the swing.'

Another influence that had to be suppressed was that of his hobby of fly-fishing that resulted in an overhead axe-swinging technique that was more akin to casting a line than smashing through a horde of Orcs. 'I had to get all my previous life out of my head,' Billy laughs, 'and get into this business of killing all these creatures.'

What proved somewhat challenging was managing the necessary axe-swinging skills while in full armour, as Billy recalls: 'I saw a sketch of me in armour and I thought, "My God, is that me?", and couldn't wait to get into it. But once I'd *got* into it, I couldn't wait to get *out* of it again! It was so heavy. "How is it?" asked Weta Workshop's Richard Taylor, and I said, "It's like wearing a small European car!" Richard explained it was made up of a lot of light layers, one on top of the other, and I just wanted to say, "Yeah, well, that's how heavy things happen. It isn't the lightness of the layers, it's the *number* of the layers." Fortunately, I kind of *like* to overheat; after all, if you're fighting you

OPPOSITE: *Early prop design by Weta Workshop of Dáin's crested helmet.* ABOVE: *Billy Connolly and Peter Jackson stand on set discussing exactly what kind of character the Scottish actor will be playing.*

should be getting hot. So, I just cook away merrily and let the sweat blind me because the more distraught you get, the more authentic it looks – or it certainly feels that way.'

Dáin's boar-riding was simulated on the green-screen stage with the actor astride a green barrel-shaped object that would later be replaced with the CG animal. 'It worked by computer,' remembers Billy, 'and it was brilliant. While I was making a speech, it shuffled around like a horse does when it's waiting to move off; and then, when I started riding, it went into a trot. I was on it for hours and while getting on wasn't a problem, getting off definitely *was* because I'd get cramp from sitting with my legs so far apart, so the stunt men would have to help me dismount. It was ridiculous and great fun: four or five guys would grab me – screaming and shouting – and I'd be bodily heaved off horizontally and then put back up into the vertical position.'

Billy Connolly has one especially treasured moment from the filming. It was when, at the end of a scene, Peter Jackson told the cast that it was time for the Dwarves' Anthem. 'I thought, "*What?* Nobody told me about any Dwarf Anthem," and then they all started singing, "Heigh-ho! Heigh-ho! It's off to work we go!"'

Steve McMichael, Swordmaster & Fight Choreographer
FiGHTiNG TALK!

'**M**Y FIRST THOUGHT,' SAYS SWORDMASTER AND FIGHT CHOREOGRAPHER, STEVE MCMICHAEL, 'WAS "HOW AM I GOING TO DO ALL THIS?" I VIVIDLY REMEMBER LOOKING AT THE LIST OF ARMAMENTS WHEN I FIRST ARRIVED ON *THE HOBBIT* AND BEING ABSOLUTELY DUMBFOUNDED BY JUST HOW MANY WEAPONS THE DWARVES CARRIED OR HAD STRAPPED TO THEIR PERSONS, ALL OF WHICH WERE COMPLETELY DIFFERENT.'

Steve also realized that his approach to weapons-handling had to take into account how each actor moved: 'They all have their own individual style, so part of the Dwarf training process was about finding something in their own personality that could be applied to their character. For example, if an actor were a squash player, I would use their ability to deliver a forehand smash to their advantage when it came to handling their weapon. It was quite a task figuring all these things out.'

Working with Movement Coach, Terry Notary, Steve established fighting moves for all the characters, even an occasional (and usually accidental) combatant like Bilbo Baggins. 'Martin Freeman also has his own specific way of moving and we always needed to take into account his unique "Bilbo-isms" as we called them.'

Steve McMichael has led a physically challenging life since joining the US Marine Corps at the age of nineteen. A Hollywood Marine (Platoon 1003 'C' Company, San

Diego) he served in Operation Desert Storm in 1991, leaving the military the rank of sergeant. Having trained in Wushu, a sport derived from Chinese martial arts, he is credited with being the first acrobatic martial art film fighter in his present home country of Canada. He has had a long and successful career as stunt performer on dozens of films and, following a serious injury, as a Stunt Coordinator and Fight Choreographer, roles he has carried out on *The Hobbit*.

Not that his past injury has even remotely slowed down a tirelessly energetic character, who during filming for *The Battle of the Five Armies* doubled for Hugo Weaving in a dramatic swordfight with the Ringwraiths at Dol Guldur.

As a highly trained expert, Steve is full of praise for the film actors' willingness to grapple with the often-gruelling demands of the action scenes in the trilogy – especially the two Elf-actors. 'Tauriel's weapons are a bow and double daggers: a pair of blades that are reminiscent of the inwardly curved Nepalese *khukri* knives. I taught Evangeline Lilly how to do brandishes with them – spinning and flipping them, catching and throwing them. Evangeline was phenomenal: it was impressive to see her desire and sheer determination to learn these moves to a level of professionalism where you totally believed in her ability to fight in this way.'

With Legolas, Steve acknowledges that the process began with what had already been established about Orlando Bloom's character in *The Lord of the Rings*. There was a certain preconception of how his character was going to look and act and, even though this is a prequel to *Rings*, I had to remain true to that. However, because Legolas is younger in *The Hobbit*, Peter Jackson let us put

in a couple of extra elements and the result is very dynamic.'

One of Steve's favourite scenes in *The Desolation of Smaug* featured Tauriel and Legolas fighting Orcs in Bard's house in Lake-town. 'We had Orlando dropping through ceilings, Evangeline blowing through doors and doing wall crawls! Basically, they did all their own stunts and it was hats off to them for what they achieved.'

Steve has particular praise for veteran Bill Connolly's efforts in rising to the task of being the Dwarf warrior, Dáin Ironfoot: 'It was an absolute pleasure to work with somebody who doesn't have a background in action filmmaking, and to be able to watch him embrace the challenge. I loved watching the progress made by this 70 year old man in order to be able to portray a tough, powerful, fighter of a king, wielding a substantial axe and coping with the limitations of heavy make-up and a costume with a weight that would have crushed a lesser man. Billy went above and beyond the call of duty and, as a result, holds a very special place in my heart.'

Reflecting on his work on *The Hobbit*, Steve says: 'It has been an incredible journey and, remembering the inevitable combination of setbacks and accomplishments, it is staggering to realize that we came up with over a hundred different fight scenes that were brought to life on screen with a wonderful cast that I trained.'

OPPOSITE: *Richard Armitage, Dean O'Gorman & Aidan Turner rehearse a fight sequence with the Stunt Crew.* **ABOVE:** *Evangeline Lilly demonstrates some of Tauriel's complex fighting moves.* **RIGHT:** *Hugo Weaving as Elrond prepares to strike, using the sword-fighting skills taught to him by Steve.*

RAVENHILL

RAVENHILL IS A DEFENSIVE OUTPOST OF THE DWARVEN KINGDOM OF EREBOR, BUILT IN A STRATEGIC POSITION ON A RIDGE OF HIGH GROUND RUNNING SOUTHWARDS FROM THE LONELY MOUNTAIN AND OVERLOOKING THE VALLEY OF DALE. TOLKIEN DESCRIBES IT AS A PLACE NAMED AFTER THE RAVENS THAT ONCE LIVED THERE AND IT FEATURES IN HIS ACCOUNT OF THE BATTLE OF THE FIVE ARMIES. IN *THE HOBBIT: THE BATTLE OF THE FIVE ARMIES*, RAVENHILL PROVIDES AN EXCITING NEW LOCATION FOR THE FILMIC VERSION OF THE BATTLE, AS PETER JACKSON EXPLAINS: 'RATHER THAN JUST HAVE ALL THE FIGHTING TAKING PLACE ON THE GENERAL BATTLEGROUND – WHICH IS ESSENTIALLY THE VALLEY BETWEEN DALE AND EREBOR – WE WANTED SOMEWHERE THAT HAD A SLIGHTLY DIFFERENT, MORE ISOLATED FEELING. SO WE CHOSE THE ANCIENT WATCHTOWER ON RAVENHILL TO BECOME AZOG'S COMMAND POST, SINCE IT PROVIDES HIM WITH A BIRD'S-EYE VIEW – IN FACT, A *RAVEN'S*-EYE VIEW – OF THE BATTLEFIELD STRETCHED OUT BEFORE HIM.'

The decision to utilize Ravenhill came about partially as a result of the inherent movie-making challenges in Tolkien's text. 'When you are trying to make a film,' says Peter, 'it is difficult to know how to convincingly interpret Tolkien's beautifully written narrative when it comes to the idea that the sudden arrival of thirteen Dwarves onto the battlefield manages to turn the tide of war. Looking at a battle involving several thousand participants, you're confronted as a filmmaker with this moment when Thorin and the others are finally going to do the right thing and burst out of the Mountain to help their brother Dwarves' struggle against the Orcs. And you ask yourself: "How do you do that?" They've got swords and axes, and they're going to kill some Orcs, but how does this change the course of the entire battle when there are so many people fighting? That's tricky! It may be easy in a book, but on film it is difficult to sell that idea to anybody.'

For Peter, the solution to that problem was Ravenhill: 'Rather than slaughter their way through thousands of Orcs, the Dwarves decide that one possible way of dealing with the enemy is to "cut the head off the snake": attempt to take out the leader in the hope that it will send the Orcs into disorganization and disarray. That is their plan, though it proves far from easy.'

Production Designer, Dan Hennah, was responsible for the design and building of the Ravenhill sets: 'Built of weathered green marble, it's an old, broken fortress standing along one of the spurs of Lonely Mountain, and has a lake, fed by the snows, that is frozen in wintertime. Because it seems to be a place of refuge, Gandalf thinks it might be somewhere to keep Bilbo out of trouble. In the event, it proves unexpectedly

OPPOSITE: *The Dwarven watchtower has fallen into ruinous disrepair.* ABOVE: *Dan Hennah and Ra Vincent ensure that figures of all the Five Armies are present in this model of Ravenhill.* RIGHT: *Graham McTavish, Richard Armitage, Dean O'Gorman & Aidan Turner stand together.* OVERLEAF: *This detailed model would be used to help guide the Digital team to create and animate the finished Ravenhill scenes.*

dangerous and a key feature of the final battlefield, which added to the complexities of the design because the various interior rooms and tunnels that the battle spills into had to look like solid rock while being "stunt friendly". Nevertheless, Ravenhill proved a great place for a battle in the middle of winter: and the frozen lake provides a pivotal encounter in the battle. There's lots of fighting on the snow, which is basically like ice hockey with swords!'

THIS PAGE: *Azog the Defiler, leader of the Orc hordes, will command his forces to the death!* OPPOSITE: *The Defiler strikes back!*

Defining the Defiler

'**A**ZOG WAS A TRICKY CHARACTER,' SAYS PETER JACKSON; 'YOU DON'T JUST HAVE AN ACTOR COME IN OFF THE STREET TO PLAY A VILLAIN AS YOU WOULD IN A JAMES BOND FILM.'

The evolution of Azog is a fascinating one. In Tolkien's Appendices to *The Lord of the Rings*, the author describes how this mighty Orc killed Thorin's grandfather, Thrór, an event that began the War of the Dwarves and Orcs. Azog was clearly a fitting villain and a powerful focus for Thorin's vengeance who could provide a sustained menace to the Dwarves and their quest throughout the cycle of films both before and after the encounter with Smaug.

Unfortunately, Tolkien's account of the Orc–Dwarf War culminates in the Battle of Azanulbizar, where Azog was slain by the Dwarf Dáin Ironfoot – who only makes his appearance in *The Hobbit* towards the end of the book. For the filmmakers this presented a dilemma and led to the decision to keep Azog alive.

'We decided,' says Philippa Boyens, 'that Thorin truly believes he has killed Azog at the Battle of Azanulbizar, but first the audience and then Thorin discovers the Orc is not dead. It is the Great Goblin who reveals the truth: in response to Thorin saying that "Azog the Defiler was destroyed; he was slain in battle long ago," the Goblin King replies, "So you think his defiling days are done, do you?" This gave us a fantastic villain.'

As Peter Jackson explains, Azog's initial appearance was quite different from the character we now know on screen: 'We started out using prosthetics and designing Azog as a wizened, decrepit old Orc. I had this idea that it could be really scary to see an Orc who looks like a wrinkled little old man when in fact he's actually a powerful force of sheer evil.'

Footage was filmed featuring this version of Azog but, increasingly, Peter realized that the portrayal wasn't conveying the threat and danger of the character in the way that the screenplay required.

'We couldn't do much about it,' recalls Peter, 'because we were in the middle of shooting the movie, so we waited till we had got the film shot and, at that point, decided we needed Azog to be a digital creature. It was certainly no fault of the actor, but this decision immediately freed us from the constraints of prosthetic make-up. We wanted him to be highly agile and very expressive and – having done Gollum and King Kong and various other digital creatures – the idea of making a digital Azog was kind of exciting and, ultimately, enabled us to create a being who was truly terrifying.'

Manu Bennett

AZOG

'**I**T WAS LIKE I HAD BEEN ABDUCTED BY ALIENS! I WAS BEING SPOKEN TO IN A DIFFERENT LANGUAGE AND GIVEN DIRECTIVES THAT WERE OUTSIDE MY KNOWLEDGE PARAMETERS.' MANU BENNETT IS TALKING ABOUT UNEXPECTEDLY FINDING HIMSELF ON A MOTION-CAPTURE SOUND STAGE IN THE LATTER MONTHS OF 2012, LEARNING HOW TO PLAY THE TOWERING MASS OF ONE-ARMED, PALE-SKINNED, BLUE-EYED EVIL THAT IS AZOG, THE ORC CHIEFTAIN OMINOUSLY KNOWN AS THE DEFILER.

Based on a character from Tolkien's legendarium and developed by Peter Jackson for *The Hobbit* trilogy, Azog had, many years earlier at a great battle before the doors of Moria, begun the War of the Dwarves and Orcs by slaying and decapitating King Thrór. In the film version of the story he would lose his left arm to the king's enraged grandson, Thorin Oakenshield.

'The first time I saw Azog,' says Manu, 'was when I got put into this funny outfit with little balls all over me, and walked out – feeling and looking like an idiot – onto the MoCap stage at Peter Jackson's Stone Street Studios. "This is what you are going to look like," they said, and up on a big screen there's this nine-foot-tall, Arnold Schwarzenegger-like monster. And I think, "Okay, so *that's* me..." And from there on in it was a voyage of discovery.'

Despite coming late to the cast of *The Hobbit*, Manu brought considerable experience from a prolific career in action film and television. Best known for his role as Crixus in the two *Spartacus* TV mini-series, *Gods of the Arena* and *War of the Damned*, Manu Bennett has also starred in such movies as *30 Days of Night*, *Sinbad and the Minotaur*, *The Marine* and *The Condemned*.

The initial intention had been for Azog to be portrayed by a performer

wearing prosthetic make-up and scenes featuring the character had been shot in that way; but, as the film progressed, it became clear that Azog's relentlessly vengeful personality required a more dynamic treatment that could only be achieved using motion-capture and digital animation. So, just a couple of months before *The Hobbit: An Unexpected Adventure* was due to premiere, Manu Bennett, who had initially been approached about the role but who was, at the time, unavailable due to his commitments on *Spartacus*, was asked to work on the project. As a result, having got compassionate leave from the amphitheatres of ancient Rome, Manu flew into Wellington to help bring the Pale Orc to life.

'The first day I arrived,' he recalls, 'I felt as if I was losing my mind. It was like, "OK, Houston, I'm putting on the space suit," and then, suddenly, I'm sucked into cyberspace, blasted into an utterly new and unknown world: a technological universe. It was fantastic, but tough: with such a tight deadline it was a matter of knuckling down and trusting to everyone's professionalism.'

Rapidly getting to grips with the demands of work on the MoCap stage, Manu began to realize the potential the unfamiliar technology offered a performer: 'You are covered in masses of little tracking dots, and surrounded by sensors, monitors and cameras that are picking up every movement you make, shooting you from above, below and all around. I'm used to performing to a single camera, but with MoCap whatever I do they've got me covered from every angle and all directions: spatially it's capturing my performance in every possible form from a master-shot to an extreme close-up and that is hugely empowering because it instantly strips you of your consciousness of being an actor.'

Exploring the potential offered by this freedom, Manu began to discover more about his character. 'You find a lot of things in performance,' he says, 'and as I got used to being on the sound stage and working through the scenes I was helped by having a semi-rendered version of what Azog would look like on a big screen. I quickly realized that if I moved at my own pace the character would look small and human, whereas he needed to move with so much more mass. Dealing with his size and strength

was one of the interesting aspects of creating the character. Each day, before filming, I'd spend about an hour just walking around the sound stage, looking at this image of him on screen and thinking, "How does he move? How does he breathe?" I had to believe that I had his physique and his lung capacity. I needed to feel like I had his great arms, that I was walking with eight-foot Orc legs and turning that massive head on the gigantic body. It was just a matter of behaving as if I were at a Mister Universe contest. Everything needed to be very big. It was no good moving like an ant, I had to move like a dinosaur. Only then could I start to capture the prowess of Azog.'

One of the drawbacks of playing a towering Orc with supernatural strengths was the necessity of having to wield a great mace. 'When I first started using the weapon,' recalls Manu, 'it was just a stick with a motion-sensor on the end of it and Peter immediately noticed that I was tending to wave it around like a wand. It simply didn't

OPPOSITE: *Manu Bennett at the LA premiere of* The Hobbit: The Desolation of Smaug. BELOW: *Azog leads his Orc army outside the East-gate of Moria.*

ABOVE: *Gandalf comes face to face with Azog.* LEFT: *The warm glow of the setting sun does not make Azog any more appealing.*

had weight and were convincing: big killing strokes delivered with great malice.'

To help visualize Azog's personality, Manu drew on various filmic inspirations: 'Two of my strongest influences were Darth Vader in *Star Wars* and, in particular, the shark in *Jaws*. Azog actually looks something like a shark: huge, sleek, threatening and muscular with vicious teeth. But the thing about *Jaws* is that you don't really see those teeth until the very last second. I had this idea that I could make Azog stealthy. With the shark it's all about that fin cruising through the water; the presence and the menace are there and then, suddenly, it explodes out of the water and comes at you! That's what I've tried to capture with Azog: that it's only at the moment of true anger and vengeance that you get to see the explosive potential of his nature.'

have any weight to it. So Pete said, "Can we put sandbags on the end of that stick?" And I thought, "Okay, I'd better warm my shoulder up!" Next time I picked it up it was really heavy and lifting and moving it around was really quite difficult. As a result my actions with the mace now

Manu went to extraordinary lengths in his determination to live out his character: 'Thorin Oakenshield cuts off Azog's left arm and, in order to try to realize the scene just a bit more convincingly, I got the guys to tape my arm up behind my back so I could experience the sense of losing an arm. At first I thought it might be a bit silly, but I discovered that if you take away the weight of one of your arms it affects the whole of that side of your body, so it was really helpful.'

In addition to the physical demands there were challenging vocal requirements as Azog uses Black Speech, the accursed language fashioned by Sauron and spoken by his servants. Manu learned the guttural tongue phonetically with help from Dialect Coach, Leith McPherson: 'It was rather like trying to learn German in ten minutes! Because the way that the words are written is not necessarily the way they sound, we took them apart and wrote them out phonetically on sheets of paper; these were set up around the studio so they were always in my eye-line wherever my character was looking.'

Leith provided Manu with a rather different form of assistance for the sequence in which Azog kills Yazneg, one of his Orcs: 'I appreciated Leith's help with the dialogue so much that I asked her to come in and play Yazneg. I had to go up to Yazneg, stroke his forehead and give him a little pat, as if everything was okay, and then pick him up by the throat and toss his body to the pack of Wargs. Poor Leith was kneeling down in front of me and became the recipient of Azog's fury. I remember saying, "Leith, I'm going to have to grab you around the throat. Is that okay?" and she said, "Manu, just do whatever it takes." So there I am, roaring with rage and throwing my dialogue coach to the jaws of the waiting Wargs.'

Azog's white Warg was, in Manu's reality, a primitive relative of the bucking bull attractions that can be encountered at fairgrounds, as the actor recalls: 'I had two stunt guys, Shane Dawson and Augie Davis, at either end of this thing and Fran Walsh was yelling, "Okay, now the Warg's going crazy!" and they're wheeling it around like an out-of-control helicopter!'

However disorientating the experience, it was, Manu confesses, the beginning of a beautiful relationship. 'We were filming the scene where Azog is seated on the white Warg with Thorin, Gandalf and the others up in the branches of the pine trees and I asked Peter, "Can I have a relationship with my Warg?" I think he wondered what I was suggesting, but I explained that it would help my performance if I could imagine that there was a subtle bond between the Orc and his ride. In this particular scene I had the line, "Do you smell it? The scent of fear?" so I asked Peter whether, instead of just directing that question at my fellow Orcs, I could run my hand through the bristling hair on the neck of my Warg and say the line as if I were asking the creature if it could smell the Dwarves' fear? Peter said, "Yeah, let's give it a go." After all, once Azog had dealt with Thorin it was likely to be dinner time for the old white Warg.'

The moment is one of which Manu Bennett is proud: 'It's a tiny detail that helps humanize – or, I suppose, "Orc-ize" – Azog's character. Since I wanted a relationship with my Warg, Peter started referring to it as "Susan", and we came up with this saying: "An Orc's best friend is his Warg." Well, if the Lone Ranger can have his Silver then why shouldn't Azog have his Susan?'

THE WETA WAY

FOR TWENTY YEARS THE SPECIAL EFFECTS MAGICIANS AT WETA WORKSHOP AND WETA DIGITAL HAVE BEEN RESPONSIBLE FOR CREATING THE ONSCREEN MAGIC IN DOZENS OF MOVIES, INCLUDING *THE LORD OF THE RINGS* AND *THE HOBBIT* TRILOGIES. AT THE END OF THEIR EXTENDED SOJOURN IN MIDDLE-EARTH, RICHARD TAYLOR, CO-FOUNDER AND DIRECTOR OF WETA WORKSHOP, AND JOE LETTERI, DIRECTOR AND SENIOR VISUAL EFFECTS SUPERVISOR OF WETA DIGITAL – BOTH FOUR-TIMES ACADEMY AWARD-WINNERS – REFLECT ON THEIR EPIC JOURNEY THERE AND BACK AGAIN...

RICHARD TAYLOR: With the huge outpouring of energy and effort, focus and dedication over the past five years we conclude – or have begun to close the doors on – this chapter in our professional lives. We can now comfortably move on to new things, knowing that we have given Tolkien's legacy and Peter's vision the absolute maximum that a group of people can give.

For me, it's been about the journey, never about the destination and as we reach the end of our fourteen years in the arena of Middle-earth, there is a sense of satisfaction borne, primarily, out of camaraderie.

I'm thrilled that the movies are beautiful and I'm thrilled that they are enjoyed by the audiences of the world, but your determination is tried and tested in the trenches.

It's tested by how you work with your colleagues, how you carry yourself under extreme pressure, because you can never really test the mettle of a fellow worker until you're with them between the hours of three and six in the morning! Everything else up until that point can be an act, but those are the moments of truth.

I reflect on how solidly and dependably everyone has carried themselves through these years with such unbridled fervour and tenacity. The fact that we've created an environment at Weta Workshop that engenders this level of comradeship and passion and delivers everyone out at the end of it – maybe a little bruised but, hopefully, otherwise unscathed – is a tremendous achievement and definitely something to celebrate.

JOE LETTERI: If I had to pick one accomplishment out of all of the things Weta Digital have achieved, I think – as much as I love Smaug – I would have to go back to Gollum. What I'm really proud of is the fact that we took a non-human, what typically you would think of as a creature, and succeeded in turning him into a character, someone with whom audiences could, and did, engage.

Gollum, to me, has withstood the test of time. Just remembering back to those early days of thinking, 'My God, how are we going to do this?', through that lengthy process of evolution to the character that we saw in *An Unexpected Journey*, and to bring Gollum back for that unforgettable one-on-one dialogue scene with Bilbo, where you really got to appreciate him as a character, was a truly satisfying way to revisit Middle-earth.

What's been so very exciting for me, working on these films, is having this vast canvas of Middle-earth that has allowed us to journey to so many different places,

and imagine and interpret so many wonderful and fantastical ideas – Elves and Dwarves, Wizards and battles – with which we all grew up.

We've achieved the ability to create the characters and creatures that believably inhabit Tolkien's world in such a way that it's not just a case of painting a picture, so much as making it come alive. That has been unique and, for me, the best part of this remarkable experience.

OPPOSITE: *Richard Taylor oversees the last detail of Gloin's helmet* (left); *just some of the thousands of items constructed by Weta Workshop* (right). **ABOVE:** *Joe Letteri* (right) *receives an update from Eric Saindon.* **RIGHT:** *Thanks to Weta Digital, Gollum is as real as Bilbo.*

BACK TO BAG END

THE SUBTITLE OF THE ORIGINAL BOOK, *THERE AND BACK AGAIN*, GIVES A CLUE TO THE ULTIMATE DESTINATION IN THE FINAL PART OF *THE HOBBIT* TRILOGY: NONE OTHER THAN BAG END, HOBBITON IN THE SHIRE!

First created for *The Lord of the Rings*, this idyllic setting with its peaceful, rural charm and its delightfully eccentric hobbit-hole houses with their round doors and windows charmed moviegoers and instantly became a symbol of everything that was being threatened by the forces of the Dark Lord, Sauron, and that Frodo and the Fellowship of the Ring were fighting to defend.

The location, as is now widely known, was the Alexander family farm just outside the Waikato town of Matamata. The appeal to the film's location scout was obvious: although only ten minutes from State Highway 1, the farm offered 360-degree vistas of lush green rolling meadowlands, unspoiled by roads, buildings, power lines or anything else other than 14,000 sheep and a few hundred head of cattle.

Russell Alexander remembers the conversation with his father, Ian, which would eventually change the course of life for the family and bring about one of the most beloved

OPPOSITE: *This aerial shot reveals the lush green meadowlands of the Alexander family farm.* ABOVE: *Bag End in the Shire: created by J.R.R. Tolkien in England, filmed by Peter Jackson in New Zealand!*

movie sets of all time: 'They said they wanted to make a movie but wouldn't reveal what it was until we had signed confidentiality papers. Then they told us that it was *The Lord of the Rings*. I'd read the book at school and knew a bit about it but my father – and he'd probably rather I didn't tell this story – said, "The Lord of the *what*?" and I quietly kicked him under the table! So, that's how it all started.'

After resolving a few important questions – such as how an operating farm would be able to function while being invaded by a three-ring circus of filmmakers – a deal was signed, the New Zealand army installed an access road and, in December 1999, cameras began rolling in Hobbiton.

Movie sets are part of the illusion of cinema: they are fleeting creations not built to last beyond the moment when the director calls 'That's a wrap!' So, when the Hobbiton scenes were in the can, the plywood and polystyrene facades to the hobbit-holes were dismantled and the circus left town.

However, such was the impact made by the opening and closing sequences of the *Rings* trilogy that tourists eager to visit the locations made famous by the films were soon beating a path to the Alexander farm and asking to see Bag End and the other hobbit dwellings. Though nothing more than slabs of concrete with round holes in them embedded in the hillside, people happily posed outside Mr Baggins' former home, pleased to be able to get even that close to a little movie magic.

When plans began to get underway for the making of *The Hobbit*, the Alexander Farm once again became crucial to the new project. Hobbiton would have to be rebuilt but, this time, Peter Jackson decided it would be constructed out of real brick and wood so that the village could remain on show for as long as people are interested in hobbits.

The Russell family endured the disruption of another movie shoot and are now back at work – running a farm *and* a tourist attraction. 'My dad,' says Russell Alexander, 'may not have known anything about *The Lord of the Rings* back in 1998, but he certainly knows about it now!'

EAST, WEST, HOME'S BEST

A thread that runs through *The Hobbit* is the concept of 'home' and its importance to the various peoples of Middle-earth: there are Rivendell, the Last Homely House, Mirkwood, the Elves' Woodland Realm and Lake-town – each anxiously concerned about the security and safety of their inhabitants; Erebor, the lost home of the Dwarves and, of course, Bilbo's own home on the Hill in Hobbit-across-the-Water.

'The idea of "home" and, with it, an awareness of identity,' says Philippa Boyens, 'is to be found in the little corners and pockets of the book. When, for example, Bilbo tumbles out of his front door of Bag End and sets out on his adventure, he carries with him a sense of not just belonging somewhere but also of longing to be back in that place. He has such strong and powerful memories of his own home that it helps him understand the Dwarves and their feelings of being dispossessed from their homeland. And, perhaps more than anything, it is thoughts of home and the hope of one day returning there that give him the courage and strength to do what has to be done.'

EPILOGUE

I N LOOKING BACK ACROSS THE FIVE YEARS DEVOTED TO MAKING *THE HOBBIT* TRILOGY, PETER JACKSON PERHAPS INEVITABLY FINDS HIMSELF LOOKING BACK ACROSS MANY MORE YEARS – TO 2001 AND THE RELEASE OF *THE LORD OF THE RINGS: THE FELLOWSHIP OF THE RING* AND, BEYOND THAT, TO EVENTS IN THE LATE 1990S: 'WE ARE MAKING FILMS IN THIS MODERN AGE OF CINEMATIC FRANCHISES AND, WHILST TOLKIEN IS THE FURTHEST THING YOU COULD IMAGINE FROM A MOVIE FRANCHISE, IN THE WAY HOLLYWOOD VIEWS ITSELF, THAT IT IS WHAT IT HAS BECOME. AS SOON AS *THE FELLOWSHIP OF THE RING* WAS A SUCCESS, THE FATE OF *THE HOBBIT* AS A FILM PROJECT HAD BEEN DECIDED. THE BOX OFFICE RETURNS ON *FELLOWSHIP* ARE THE REASON WHY WE ARE WHERE WE ARE NOW.'

In 1995, Peter had proposed a project to Harvey Weinstein of Miramax films: a film based on *The Hobbit* and, if it was successful, a two-picture version of *The Lord of the Rings*. 'I've thought a lot,' says Peter, 'about what that *Hobbit* movie might have been like if we had made it before *The Lord of the Rings*. And, you know, I'm glad it didn't work out like that, because if Harvey had said, "Yes, that's great, no problem, let's do it," then *The Hobbit* would have been a very different film to the one that we have now made.

'Tolkien frequently brushes over major events very quickly and with little or no detail, and I think that the truth is, if you made a single film that truly follows the narrative of *The Hobbit*, people would find it rather juvenile and shallow. Ultimately, it would feel like a film maybe of the 1930s but really not of the modern day for audiences who have expectations of so much more in terms of drama, action and character development. So, yes, we've embellished the original story in places and, in other places have added in bits and pieces from Tolkien's Appendices to *The Lord of the Rings*, but we are being reasonably faithful to the narrative of *The Hobbit* and the result is simply what we feel it needs to be.'

The tone of Tolkien's first book would most certainly

have presented difficulties for filmmakers who were required to try and tie in *The Hobbit* with *The Lord of the Rings*: 'To have the charming, whimsical, simple narrative of a children's book crashing into the epic drama of the *Rings* trilogy would not have worked. As it is, I think that has also served us well, because we've ended up with six movies that stylistically have a true unity.'

And that unity has, in turn, affected how future generations will respond to *The Lord of the Rings*, as Peter explains: 'In a few years' time, there will be audiences for these films who won't have any memory or knowledge of which were made first and, hence, no preconceptions; they'll simply be watching them in the order that the story demands – from number one through to number six.'

That is a concept that Peter Jackson finds especially satisfying: 'It was a joy for us to go back and to tell a completely different story while, at the same time, having a lot of fun weaving in characters, story threads and set-ups that ultimately pay off in *The Lord of the Rings* – something we could never have done if we had made *The Hobbit* first. And, as a result, I hope that when people finally sit down to watch all six films – the double-trilogy – they will have a much fuller and richer experience.'